THE EARLY SHORT FICTION OF EDITH WHARTON

BY

EDITH WHARTON

A TEN-PART COLLECTION
VOLUME TWO

British Library Cataloguing-in-Publication Data
A catalogue record for this book is available from the
British Library

CONTENTS

CONTENTS

Edith Wharton

Edith Wharton was born in New York City in 1862. Her family were extremely wealthy, and during her youth she was provided private tuition and travelled extensively in Europe. A voracious reader, Wharton studied literature, philosophy, science, and art, and began to write poetry and short fiction. In 1885, aged 23, Edith married a banker, Edward Robbins, and for the next few years they travelled extensively together. Living near Central Park in New York, Wharton's first poems were published in *Scribner's Magazine*. In 1891, the same publication printed the first of her many short stories, titled 'Mrs. Manstey's View'. Over the next four decades, they – along with other well-established American publications such as *Atlantic Monthly*, *Century Magazine*, *Harper's* and *Lippincott's* – regularly published her work.

A lifelong keen architect, in 1902 Wharton designed and built her home, The Mount, in Lenox, Massachusetts. It was while living here that she wrote many of her works, including the 1905 novel *The House of Mirth*, which was that year's bestseller, and is now considered a classic of American literary Naturalism. In the period leading up to the First World War, Wharton wrote prolifically, and in 1921 she received the Pulitzer Prize – the first ever woman to do so – for her novel *The Age of Innocence*. Like much of her work, the novel examines the tension between societal pressures and the pursuit of genuine happiness, and includes careful use of dramatic irony.

Edith Wharton died of a stroke in 1937, aged 75. In addition to her novels, she is remembered for her short fiction, especially her excellent ghost stories.

AFTERWARD

January 1910

CHAPTER I

"Oh, there IS one, of course, but you'll never know it."

The assertion, laughingly flung out six months earlier in a bright June garden, came back to Mary Boyne with a sharp perception of its latent significance as she stood, in the December dusk, waiting for the lamps to be brought into the library.

The words had been spoken by their friend Alida Stair, as they sat at tea on her lawn at Pangbourne, in reference to the very house of which the library in question was the central, the pivotal "feature." Mary Boyne and her husband, in quest of a country place in one of the southern or southwestern counties, had, on their arrival in England, carried their problem straight to Alida Stair, who had successfully solved it in her own case; but it was not until they had rejected, almost capriciously, several practical and judicious suggestions that she threw it out: "Well, there's Lyng, in Dorsetshire. It belongs to Hugo's cousins, and you can get it for a song."

The reasons she gave for its being obtainable on these terms—its remoteness from a station, its lack of electric light, hot-water pipes, and other vulgar necessities—were exactly those pleading in its favor with two romantic Americans perversely in search of the economic drawbacks which were associated, in their tradition, with unusual architectural felicities.

"I should never believe I was living in an old house unless I was thoroughly uncomfortable," Ned Boyne, the more extravagant of the two, had jocosely insisted; "the least hint of 'convenience' would make me think it had been bought out of an exhibition, with the pieces numbered, and set up again." And they had proceeded to enumerate, with humorous precision, their various suspicions and exactions, refusing to believe that the house their cousin recommended was REALLY Tudor till they learned it had no heating system, or that the village church was literally in the grounds till she assured them of the deplorable uncertainty of the water-supply.

"It's too uncomfortable to be true!" Edward Boyne had continued to exult as the avowal of each disadvantage was successively wrung from her; but he had cut short his rhapsody to ask, with a sudden relapse to distrust: "And the ghost? You've been concealing from us the fact that there is no ghost!"

Mary, at the moment, had laughed with him, yet almost with her laugh, being possessed of several sets of independent perceptions, had noted a sudden flatness of tone in Alida's answering hilarity.

"Oh, Dorsetshire's full of ghosts, you know."

"Yes, yes; but that won't do. I don't want to have to drive ten miles to see somebody else's ghost. I want one of my own on the premises. IS there a ghost at Lyng?"

His rejoinder had made Alida laugh again, and it was then that she had flung back tantalizingly: "Oh, there IS one, of course, but you'll never know it."

"Never know it?" Boyne pulled her up. "But what in the world constitutes a ghost except the fact of its being known for one?"

"I can't say. But that's the story."

"That there's a ghost, but that nobody knows it's a ghost?"

"Well—not till afterward, at any rate."

"Till afterward?"

"Not till long, long afterward."

"But if it's once been identified as an unearthly visitant, why hasn't its signalement been handed down in the family? How has it managed to preserve its incognito?"

Alida could only shake her head. "Don't ask me. But it has."

"And then suddenly—" Mary spoke up as if from some cavernous depth of divination—"suddenly, long afterward, one says to one's self, 'THAT WAS it?'"

She was oddly startled at the sepulchral sound with which her question fell on the banter of the other two, and she saw the shadow of the same surprise flit across Alida's clear pupils. "I suppose so. One just has to wait."

"Oh, hang waiting!" Ned broke in. "Life's too short for a ghost who can only be enjoyed in retrospect. Can't we do better than that, Mary?"

But it turned out that in the event they were not destined to, for within three months of their conversation with Mrs. Stair they were established at Lyng, and the life they had yearned for to the point of planning it out in all its daily details had actually begun for them.

It was to sit, in the thick December dusk, by just such a wide-hooded fireplace, under just such black oak rafters, with the sense that beyond the mullioned panes the downs were darkening to a deeper solitude: it was for the ultimate indulgence in such sensations that Mary Boyne had endured for nearly fourteen years the soul-deadening ugliness of the Middle West, and that Boyne had ground on doggedly at his engineering till, with a suddenness that still made her blink, the prodigious windfall of the Blue Star Mine had put them at a stroke in possession of life and the leisure to taste it. They had never for a moment meant their new state to be one of idleness; but they meant to give themselves only to harmonious activities. She had her vision of painting and gardening (against a background of gray walls), he dreamed of the production of his long-planned book on the "Economic Basis of Culture"; and with such absorbing work ahead no existence could be too sequestered; they could not get far enough from the world, or plunge deep enough into the past.

Dorsetshire had attracted them from the first by a semblance of remoteness out of all proportion to its geographical position. But to the Boynes it was one of the ever-recurring wonders of the whole incredibly compressed island—a nest of counties, as they put it—that for the production of its effects so little of a given quality went so far: that so few miles made a distance, and so short a distance a difference.

"It's that," Ned had once enthusiastically explained, "that gives such depth to their effects, such relief to their least contrasts. They've been able to lay the butter so thick on every exquisite mouthful."

The butter had certainly been laid on thick at Lyng: the old gray house, hidden under a shoulder of the downs, had almost all the finer marks of commerce with a protracted past. The mere fact that it was neither large nor exceptional made it, to the Boynes, abound the more richly in its special sense—the sense of having been for centuries a deep, dim reservoir of life. The life had probably not been of the most vivid order: for long periods, no doubt, it had fallen as noiselessly into the past as the quiet drizzle of autumn fell, hour after hour, into the green fish-pond between the yews; but these back-waters of existence sometimes breed, in their sluggish depths, strange acuities of emotion, and

Mary Boyne had felt from the first the occasional brush of an intenser memory.

The feeling had never been stronger than on the December afternoon when, waiting in the library for the belated lamps, she rose from her seat and stood among the shadows of the hearth. Her husband had gone off, after luncheon, for one of his long tramps on the downs. She had noticed of late that he preferred to be unaccompanied on these occasions; and, in the tried security of their personal relations, had been driven to conclude that his book was bothering him, and that he needed the afternoons to turn over in solitude the problems left from the morning's work. Certainly the book was not going as smoothly as she had imagined it would, and the lines of perplexity between his eyes had never been there in his engineering days. Then he had often looked fagged to the verge of illness, but the native demon of "worry" had never branded his brow. Yet the few pages he had so far read to her—the introduction, and a synopsis of the opening chapter—gave evidences of a firm possession of his subject, and a deepening confidence in his powers.

The fact threw her into deeper perplexity, since, now that he had done with "business" and its disturbing contingencies, the one other possible element of anxiety was eliminated. Unless it were his health, then? But physically he had gained since they had come to Dorsetshire, grown robuster, ruddier, and fresher-eyed. It was only within a week that she had felt in him the undefinable change that made her restless in his absence, and as tongue-tied in his presence as though it were SHE who had a secret to keep from him!

The thought that there WAS a secret somewhere between them struck her with a sudden smart rap of wonder, and she looked about her down the dim, long room.

"Can it be the house?" she mused.

The room itself might have been full of secrets. They seemed to be piling themselves up, as evening fell, like the layers and layers of velvet shadow dropping from the low ceiling, the dusky walls of books, the smoke-blurred sculpture of the hooded hearth.

"Why, of course—the house is haunted!" she reflected.

The ghost—Alida's imperceptible ghost—after figuring largely in the banter of their first month or two at Lyng, had been gradually discarded as too ineffectual for imaginative use. Mary had, indeed, as became the tenant of a haunted house, made the customary inquiries among her few rural neighbors, but, beyond a vague, "They du say so, Ma'am," the villagers had nothing to impart. The elusive specter had apparently never had sufficient identity for a legend to crystallize about it, and after a time the Boynes had laughingly set the matter down to their profit-and-loss account, agreeing that Lyng was one of the few houses good enough in itself to dispense with supernatural enhancements.

"And I suppose, poor, ineffectual demon, that's why it beats its beautiful wings in vain in the void," Mary had laughingly concluded.

"Or, rather," Ned answered, in the same strain, "why, amid so much that's ghostly, it can never affirm its separate existence as THE ghost." And thereupon their invisible housemate had finally dropped out of their references, which were numerous enough to make them promptly unaware of the loss.

Now, as she stood on the hearth, the subject of their earlier curiosity revived in her with a new sense of its meaning—a sense gradually acquired through close daily contact with the scene of the lurking mystery. It was the house itself, of course, that possessed the ghost-seeing faculty, that communed visually but secretly with its own past; and if one could only get into close enough communion with the house, one might surprise its secret, and acquire the ghost-sight on one's own account. Perhaps, in his long solitary hours in this very room, where she never trespassed till the afternoon, her husband HAD acquired it already, and was silently carrying the dread weight of whatever it had revealed to him. Mary was too well-versed in the code of the spectral world not to know that one could not talk about the ghosts one saw: to do so was almost as great a breach of good-breeding as to name a lady in a club. But this explanation did not really satisfy her. "What, after all, except for the fun of the frisson," she reflected, "would he really care for any of their old ghosts?" And thence she was thrown back once more on the fundamental dilemma: the fact that one's greater or less susceptibility to spectral influences had no particular bearing on the case, since, when one DID see a ghost at Lyng, one did not know it.

"Not till long afterward," Alida Stair had said. Well, supposing Ned HAD seen one when they first came, and had known only within the last week what had happened to him? More and more under the spell of the hour, she threw back her searching thoughts to the early days of their tenancy, but at first only to recall a gay confusion of unpacking, settling, arranging of books, and calling to each other from remote corners of the house as treasure after treasure of their habitation revealed itself to them. It was in this particular connection that she presently recalled a certain soft afternoon of the previous October, when, passing from the first rapturous flurry of exploration to a detailed inspection of the old house, she had pressed (like a novel heroine) a panel that opened at her touch, on a narrow flight of stairs leading to an unsuspected flat ledge of the roof—the roof which, from below, seemed to slope away on all sides too abruptly for any but practised feet to scale.

The view from this hidden coign was enchanting, and she had flown down to snatch Ned from his papers and give him the freedom of her discovery. She remembered still how, standing on the narrow ledge, he had passed his arm about her while their gaze flew to the long, tossed horizon-line of the downs, and then dropped contentedly back to trace the arabesque of yew hedges about the fish-pond, and the shadow of the cedar on the lawn.

"And now the other way," he had said, gently turning her about within his arm; and closely pressed to him, she had absorbed, like some long, satisfying draft, the picture of the gray-walled court, the squat lions on the gates, and the lime-avenue reaching up to the highroad under the downs.

It was just then, while they gazed and held each other, that she had felt his arm relax, and heard a sharp "Hullo!" that made her turn to glance at him.

Distinctly, yes, she now recalled she had seen, as she glanced, a shadow of anxiety, of perplexity, rather, fall across his face; and, following his eyes, had beheld the figure of a man—a man in loose, grayish clothes, as it appeared to her—who was sauntering down the lime-avenue to the court with the tentative gait of a stranger seeking his way. Her short-sighted eyes had given her but a blurred impression of slightness and grayness, with something foreign, or at least unlocal, in the cut of the figure or its garb; but her husband had apparently seen more—seen enough to make him push past her with a sharp "Wait!" and dash down the twisting stairs without pausing to give her a hand for the descent.

A slight tendency to dizziness obliged her, after a provisional clutch at the chimney against which they had been leaning, to follow him down more cautiously; and when she had reached the attic landing she paused again for a less definite reason, leaning over the oak banister to strain her eyes through the silence of the brown, sun-flecked depths below. She lingered there till, somewhere in those depths, she heard the closing of a door; then, mechanically impelled, she went down the shallow flights of steps till she reached the lower hall.

The front door stood open on the mild sunlight of the court, and hall and court were empty. The library door was open, too, and after listening in vain for any sound of voices within, she quickly crossed the threshold, and found her husband alone, vaguely fingering the papers on his desk.

He looked up, as if surprised at her precipitate entrance, but the shadow of anxiety had passed from his face, leaving it even, as she fancied, a little brighter and clearer than usual.

"What was it? Who was it?" she asked.

"Who?" he repeated, with the surprise still all on his side.

"The man we saw coming toward the house."

He seemed honestly to reflect. "The man? Why, I thought I saw Peters; I dashed after him to say a word about the stable-drains, but he had disappeared before I could get down."

"Disappeared? Why, he seemed to be walking so slowly when we saw him."

Boyne shrugged his shoulders. "So I thought; but he must have got up steam in the interval. What do you say to our trying a scramble up Meldon Steep before sunset?"

That was all. At the time the occurrence had been less than nothing, had, indeed, been immediately obliterated by the magic of their first vision from Meldon Steep, a height which they had dreamed of climbing ever since they had first seen its bare spine heaving itself above the low roof of Lyng. Doubtless it was the mere fact of the other incident's having occurred on the very day of their ascent to Meldon that had kept it stored away in the unconscious fold of association from which it now emerged; for in itself it had no mark of the portentous. At the moment there could have been nothing more natural than that Ned should dash himself from the roof in the pursuit of dilatory tradesmen. It was the period when they were always on the watch for one or the other of the specialists employed about the place; always lying in wait for them, and dashing out at them with questions, reproaches, or reminders. And certainly in the distance the gray figure had looked like Peters.

Yet now, as she reviewed the rapid scene, she felt her husband's explanation of it to have been invalidated by the look of anxiety on his face. Why had the familiar appearance of Peters made him anxious? Why, above all, if it was of such prime necessity to confer with that authority on the subject of the stable-drains, had the failure to find him produced such a look of relief? Mary could not say that any one of these considerations had occurred to her at the time, yet, from the promptness with which they now marshaled themselves at her summons, she had a sudden sense that they must all along have been there, waiting their hour.

CHAPTER II

Weary with her thoughts, she moved toward the window. The library was now completely dark, and she was surprised to see how much faint light the outer world still held.

As she peered out into it across the court, a figure shaped itself in the tapering perspective of bare lines: it looked a mere blot of deeper gray in the grayness, and for an instant, as it moved toward her, her heart thumped to the thought, "It's the ghost!"

She had time, in that long instant, to feel suddenly that the man of whom, two months earlier, she had a brief distant vision from the roof was now, at his predestined hour, about to reveal himself as NOT having been Peters; and her spirit sank under the impending fear of the disclosure. But almost with the next tick of the clock the ambiguous figure, gaining substance and character, showed itself even to her weak sight as her husband's; and she turned away to meet him, as he entered, with the confession of her folly.

"It's really too absurd," she laughed out from the threshold, "but I never CAN remember!"

"Remember what?" Boyne questioned as they drew together.

"That when one sees the Lyng ghost one never knows it."

Her hand was on his sleeve, and he kept it there, but with no response in his gesture or in the lines of his fagged, preoccupied face.

"Did you think you'd seen it?" he asked, after an appreciable interval.

"Why, I actually took YOU for it, my dear, in my mad determination to spot it!"

"Me—just now?" His arm dropped away, and he turned from her with a faint echo of her laugh. "Really, dearest, you'd better give it up, if that's the best you can do."

"Yes, I give it up—I give it up. Have YOU?" she asked, turning round on him abruptly.

The parlor-maid had entered with letters and a lamp, and the light struck up into Boyne's face as he bent above the tray she presented.

"Have YOU?" Mary perversely insisted, when the servant had disappeared on her errand of illumination.

"Have I what?" he rejoined absently, the light bringing out the sharp stamp of worry between his brows as he turned over the letters.

"Given up trying to see the ghost." Her heart beat a little at the experiment she was making.

Her husband, laying his letters aside, moved away into the shadow of the hearth.

"I never tried," he said, tearing open the wrapper of a newspaper.

"Well, of course," Mary persisted, "the exasperating thing is that there's no use trying, since one can't be sure till so long afterward."

He was unfolding the paper as if he had hardly heard her; but after a pause, during which the sheets rustled spasmodically between his hands, he lifted his head to say abruptly, "Have you any idea HOW LONG?"

Mary had sunk into a low chair beside the fireplace. From her seat she looked up, startled, at her husband's profile, which was darkly projected against the circle of lamplight.

"No; none. Have YOU?" she retorted, repeating her former phrase with an added keenness of intention.

Boyne crumpled the paper into a bunch, and then inconsequently turned back with it toward the lamp.

"Lord, no! I only meant," he explained, with a faint tinge of impatience, "is there any legend, any tradition, as to that?"

"Not that I know of," she answered; but the impulse to add, "What makes you ask?" was checked by the reappearance of the parlor-maid with tea and a second lamp.

With the dispersal of shadows, and the repetition of the daily domestic office, Mary Boyne felt herself less oppressed by that sense of something mutely imminent which had darkened her solitary afternoon. For a few moments she gave herself silently to the details of her task, and when she looked up from it she was struck to the point of bewilderment by the change in her husband's face. He had seated himself near the farther lamp, and was absorbed in the perusal of his letters; but was it something he had found in them, or merely the shifting of her own point of view, that had restored his features to their normal aspect? The longer she looked, the more definitely the change affirmed itself. The lines of painful tension had vanished, and such traces of fatigue as lingered were of the kind easily attributable to steady mental effort. He glanced up, as if drawn by her gaze, and met her eyes with a smile.

"I'm dying for my tea, you know; and here's a letter for you," he said.

She took the letter he held out in exchange for the cup she proffered him, and, returning to her seat, broke the seal with the languid gesture of the reader whose interests are all inclosed in the circle of one cherished presence.

Her next conscious motion was that of starting to her feet, the letter falling to them as she rose, while she held out to her husband a long newspaper clipping.

"Ned! What's this? What does it mean?"

He had risen at the same instant, almost as if hearing her cry before she uttered it; and for a perceptible space of time he and she studied each other, like adversaries watching for an advantage, across the space between her chair and his desk.

"What's what? You fairly made me jump!" Boyne said at length, moving toward her with a sudden, half-exasperated laugh. The shadow of apprehension was on his face again, not now a look of fixed foreboding, but a shifting vigilance of lips and eyes that gave her the sense of his feeling himself invisibly surrounded.

Her hand shook so that she could hardly give him the clipping.

"This article—from the 'Waukesha Sentinel'—that a man named Elwell has brought suit against you—that there was something wrong about the Blue Star Mine. I can't understand more than half."

They continued to face each other as she spoke, and to her astonishment, she saw that her words had the almost immediate effect of dissipating the strained watchfulness of his look.

"Oh, THAT!" He glanced down the printed slip, and then folded it with the gesture of one who handles something harmless and familiar. "What's the matter with you this afternoon, Mary? I thought you'd got bad news."

She stood before him with her undefinable terror subsiding slowly under the reassuring touch of his composure.

"You knew about this, then—it's all right?"

"Certainly I knew about it; and it's all right."

"But what IS it? I don't understand. What does this man accuse you of?"

"Oh, pretty nearly every crime in the calendar." Boyne had tossed the clipping down, and thrown himself comfortably into an arm-chair near the fire. "Do you want to hear the story? It's not particularly interesting—just a squabble over interests in the Blue Star."

"But who is this Elwell? I don't know the name."

"Oh, he's a fellow I put into it—gave him a hand up. I told you all about him at the time."

"I daresay. I must have forgotten." Vainly she strained back among her memories. "But if you helped him, why does he make this return?"

"Oh, probably some shyster lawyer got hold of him and talked him over. It's all rather technical and complicated. I thought that kind of thing bored you."

His wife felt a sting of compunction. Theoretically, she deprecated the American wife's detachment from her husband's professional interests, but in practice she had always found it difficult to fix her attention on Boyne's report of the transactions in which his varied interests involved him. Besides, she had felt from the first that, in a community where the amenities of living could be obtained only at the cost of efforts as arduous as her husband's professional labors, such brief leisure as they could command should be used as an escape from immediate preoccupations, a flight to the life they always dreamed of living. Once or twice, now that this new life had actually drawn its magic circle about them, she had asked herself if she had done right; but hitherto such conjectures had been no more than the retrospective excursions of an active fancy. Now, for the first time, it startled her a little to find how little she knew of the material foundation on which her happiness was built.

She glanced again at her husband, and was reassured by the composure of his face; yet she felt the need of more definite grounds for her reassurance.

"But doesn't this suit worry you? Why have you never spoken to me about it?"

He answered both questions at once: "I didn't speak of it at first because it DID worry me—annoyed me, rather. But it's all ancient history now. Your correspondent must have got hold of a back number of the 'Sentinel.'"

She felt a quick thrill of relief. "You mean it's over? He's lost his case?"

There was a just perceptible delay in Boyne's reply. "The suit's been withdrawn—that's all."

But she persisted, as if to exonerate herself from the inward charge of being too easily put off. "Withdrawn because he saw he had no chance?"

"Oh, he had no chance," Boyne answered.

She was still struggling with a dimly felt perplexity at the back of her thoughts.

"How long ago was it withdrawn?"

He paused, as if with a slight return of his former uncertainty. "I've just had the news now; but I've been expecting it."

"Just now—in one of your letters?"

"Yes; in one of my letters."

She made no answer, and was aware only, after a short

interval of waiting, that he had risen, and strolling across the room, had placed himself on the sofa at her side. She felt him, as he did so, pass an arm about her, she felt his hand seek hers and clasp it, and turning slowly, drawn by the warmth of his cheek, she met the smiling clearness of his eyes.

"It's all right—it's all right?" she questioned, through the flood of her dissolving doubts; and "I give you my word it never was righter!" he laughed back at her, holding her close.

CHAPTER III

One of the strangest things she was afterward to recall out of all the next day's incredible strangeness was the sudden and complete recovery of her sense of security.

It was in the air when she woke in her low-ceilinged, dusky room; it accompanied her down-stairs to the breakfast-table, flashed out at her from the fire, and re-duplicated itself brightly from the flanks of the urn and the sturdy flutings of the Georgian teapot. It was as if, in some roundabout way, all her diffused apprehensions of the previous day, with their moment of sharp concentration about the newspaper article,—as if this dim questioning of the future, and startled return upon the past,—had between them liquidated the arrears of some haunting moral obligation. If she had indeed been careless of her husband's affairs, it was, her new state seemed to prove, because her faith in him instinctively justified such carelessness; and his right to her faith had overwhelmingly affirmed itself in the very face of menace and suspicion. She had never seen him more untroubled, more naturally and unconsciously in possession of himself, than after the cross-examination to which she had subjected him: it was almost as if he had been aware of her lurking doubts, and had wanted the air cleared as much as she did.

It was as clear, thank Heaven! as the bright outer light that surprised her almost with a touch of summer when she issued from the house for her daily round of the gardens. She had left Boyne at his desk, indulging herself, as she passed the library door, by a last peep at his quiet face, where he bent, pipe in his mouth, above his papers, and now she had her own morning's task to perform. The task involved on such charmed winter days almost as much delighted loitering about the different quarters of her demesne as if spring were already at work on shrubs and borders. There were such inexhaustible possibilities still before her, such opportunities to bring out the latent graces of the old place, without a single irreverent touch of alteration, that the winter months were all too short to plan what spring and autumn executed. And her recovered sense of safety gave, on this particular morning, a peculiar zest to her progress through the sweet, still place. She went first to the kitchen-garden, where the espaliered pear-trees drew complicated patterns on the walls, and pigeons were fluttering and preening about the silvery-slated roof of their cot. There was something wrong about the piping of the hothouse, and she was expecting an authority from Dorchester, who was to drive out between trains and make a diagnosis of the boiler. But when she dipped into the damp heat of the greenhouses, among the spiced scents and waxy pinks and reds of old-fashioned exotics,—even the flora of Lyng was in the note!—she learned that the great man had not arrived, and the day being too rare to waste in an artificial atmosphere, she came out again and paced slowly along the springy turf of the bowling-green to the gardens behind the house. At their farther end rose a grass terrace, commanding, over the fish-pond and the yew hedges, a view of the long house-front, with its twisted chimney-stacks and the blue shadows of its roof angles, all drenched in the pale gold moisture of the air.

Seen thus, across the level tracery of the yews, under the suffused, mild light, it sent her, from its open windows and hospitably smoking chimneys, the look of some warm human presence, of a mind slowly ripened on a sunny wall of experience. She had never before had so deep a sense of her intimacy with it, such a conviction that its secrets were all beneficent, kept, as they said to children, "for one's good," so complete a trust in its power to gather up her life and Ned's into the harmonious pattern of the long, long story it sat there weaving in the sun.

She heard steps behind her, and turned, expecting to see the gardener, accompanied by the engineer from Dorchester. But only one figure was in sight, that of a youngish, slightly built man, who, for reasons she could not on the spot have specified, did not remotely resemble her preconceived notion of an authority on hot-house boilers. The new-comer, on seeing her, lifted his hat, and paused with the air of a gentleman—perhaps a traveler—desirous of having it immediately known that his intrusion is involuntary. The local fame of Lyng occasionally attracted the more intelligent sight-seer, and Mary half-expected to see the stranger dissemble a camera, or justify his presence by producing it. But he made no gesture of any sort, and after a moment she asked, in a tone responding to the courteous deprecation of his attitude: "Is there any one you wish to see?"

"I came to see Mr. Boyne," he replied. His intonation, rather than his accent, was faintly American, and Mary, at the familiar note, looked at him more closely. The brim of his soft felt hat cast a shade on his face, which, thus obscured, wore to her short-sighted gaze a look of seriousness, as of a person arriving "on business," and civilly but firmly aware of his rights.

Past experience had made Mary equally sensible to such claims; but she was jealous of her husband's morning hours, and doubtful of his having given any one the right to intrude on them.

"Have you an appointment with Mr. Boyne?" she asked.

He hesitated, as if unprepared for the question.

"Not exactly an appointment," he replied.

"Then I'm afraid, this being his working-time, that he can't receive you now. Will you give me a message, or come back later?"

The visitor, again lifting his hat, briefly replied that he would come back later, and walked away, as if to regain the front of the house. As his figure receded down the walk between the yew hedges, Mary saw him pause and look up an instant at the peaceful house-front bathed in faint winter sunshine; and it struck her, with a tardy touch of compunction, that it would have been more humane to ask if he had come from a distance, and to offer, in that case, to inquire if her husband could receive him. But as the thought occurred to her he passed out of sight behind a pyramidal yew, and at the same moment her attention was distracted by the approach of the gardener, attended by the bearded pepper-and-salt figure of the boiler-maker from Dorchester.

The encounter with this authority led to such far-reaching issues that they resulted in his finding it expedient to ignore his train, and beguiled Mary into spending the remainder of the morning in absorbed confabulation among the greenhouses. She was startled to find, when the colloquy ended, that it was nearly luncheon-time, and she half expected, as she hurried back to the house, to see her husband coming out to meet her. But she found no one in the court but an under-gardener raking the gravel, and the hall, when she entered it, was so silent that she guessed Boyne to be still at work behind the closed door of the library.

Not wishing to disturb him, she turned into the drawing-room, and there, at her writing-table, lost herself in renewed calculations of the outlay to which the morning's conference had committed her. The knowledge that she could permit herself such follies had not yet lost its novelty; and somehow, in contrast to the vague apprehensions of the previous days, it now seemed an element of her recovered security, of the sense that, as Ned had said, things in general had never been "righter."

She was still luxuriating in a lavish play of figures when the parlor-maid, from the threshold, roused her with a dubiously worded inquiry as to the expediency of serving luncheon. It was one of their jokes that Trimmle announced luncheon as if she were divulging a state secret, and Mary, intent upon her papers, merely murmured an absent-minded assent.

She felt Trimmle wavering expressively on the threshold as if in rebuke of such offhand acquiescence; then her retreating steps sounded down the passage, and Mary, pushing away her papers, crossed the hall, and went to the library door. It was still closed, and she wavered in her turn, disliking to disturb her husband, yet anxious that he should not exceed his normal measure of work. As she stood there, balancing her impulses, the esoteric Trimmle returned with the announcement of luncheon, and Mary, thus impelled, opened the door and went into the library.

Boyne was not at his desk, and she peered about her, expecting to discover him at the book-shelves, somewhere down the length of the room; but her call brought no response, and gradually it became clear to her that he was not in the library.

She turned back to the parlor-maid.

"Mr. Boyne must be up-stairs. Please tell him that luncheon

is ready."

The parlor-maid appeared to hesitate between the obvious duty of obeying orders and an equally obvious conviction of the foolishness of the injunction laid upon her. The struggle resulted in her saying doubtfully, "If you please, Madam, Mr. Boyne's not up-stairs."

"Not in his room? Are you sure?"

"I'm sure, Madam."

Mary consulted the clock. "Where is he, then?"

"He's gone out," Trimmle announced, with the superior air of one who has respectfully waited for the question that a well-ordered mind would have first propounded.

Mary's previous conjecture had been right, then. Boyne must have gone to the gardens to meet her, and since she had missed him, it was clear that he had taken the shorter way by the south door, instead of going round to the court. She crossed the hall to the glass portal opening directly on the yew garden, but the parlor-maid, after another moment of inner conflict, decided to bring out recklessly, "Please, Madam, Mr. Boyne didn't go that way."

Mary turned back. "Where DID he go? And when?"

"He went out of the front door, up the drive, Madam." It was a matter of principle with Trimmle never to answer more than one question at a time.

"Up the drive? At this hour?" Mary went to the door herself, and glanced across the court through the long tunnel of bare limes. But its perspective was as empty as when she had scanned it on entering the house.

"Did Mr. Boyne leave no message?" she asked.

Trimmle seemed to surrender herself to a last struggle with the forces of chaos.

"No, Madam. He just went out with the gentleman."

"The gentleman? What gentleman?" Mary wheeled about, as if to front this new factor.

"The gentleman who called, Madam," said Trimmle, resignedly.

"When did a gentleman call? Do explain yourself, Trimmle!"

Only the fact that Mary was very hungry, and that she wanted to consult her husband about the greenhouses, would have caused her to lay so unusual an injunction on her attendant; and even now she was detached enough to note in Trimmle's eye the dawning defiance of the respectful subordinate who has been pressed too hard.

"I couldn't exactly say the hour, Madam, because I didn't let the gentleman in," she replied, with the air of magnanimously ignoring the irregularity of her mistress's course.

"You didn't let him in?"

"No, Madam. When the bell rang I was dressing, and Agnes—"

"Go and ask Agnes, then," Mary interjected. Trimmle still wore her look of patient magnanimity. "Agnes would not know, Madam, for she had unfortunately burnt her hand in trying the wick of the new lamp from town—" Trimmle, as Mary was aware, had always been opposed to the new lamp— "and so Mrs. Dockett sent the kitchen-maid instead."

Mary looked again at the clock. "It's after two! Go and ask the kitchen-maid if Mr. Boyne left any word."

She went into luncheon without waiting, and Trimmle presently brought her there the kitchen-maid's statement that the gentleman had called about one o'clock, that Mr. Boyne had gone out with him without leaving any message. The kitchen-maid did not even know the caller's name, for he had written it on a slip of paper, which he had folded and handed to her, with the injunction to deliver it at once to Mr. Boyne.

Mary finished her luncheon, still wondering, and when it was over, and Trimmle had brought the coffee to the drawing-room, her wonder had deepened to a first faint tinge of disquietude. It was unlike Boyne to absent himself without explanation at so unwonted an hour, and the difficulty of identifying the visitor whose summons he had apparently obeyed made his disappearance the more unaccountable. Mary Boyne's experience as the wife of a busy engineer, subject to sudden calls and compelled to keep irregular hours, had trained her to the philosophic acceptance of surprises; but since Boyne's withdrawal from business he had adopted a Benedictine regularity of life. As if to make up for the dispersed and agitated years, with their "stand-up" lunches and dinners rattled down to the joltings of the dining-car, he cultivated the last refinements of punctuality and monotony, discouraging his wife's fancy for the unexpected; and declaring that to a delicate taste there were infinite gradations of pleasure in the fixed recurrences of habit.

Still, since no life can completely defend itself from the unforeseen, it was evident that all Boyne's precautions would sooner or later prove unavailable, and Mary concluded that he had cut short a tiresome visit by walking with his caller to the station, or at least accompanying him for part of the way.

This conclusion relieved her from farther preoccupation, and she went out herself to take up her conference with the gardener. Thence she walked to the village post-office, a mile or so away; and when she turned toward home, the early twilight was setting in.

She had taken a foot-path across the downs, and as Boyne, meanwhile, had probably returned from the station by the highroad, there was little likelihood of their meeting on the way. She felt sure, however, of his having reached the house before her; so sure that, when she entered it herself, without even pausing to inquire of Trimmle, she made directly for the library. But the library was still empty, and with an unwonted precision of visual memory she immediately observed that the papers on her husband's desk lay precisely as they had lain when she had gone in to call him to luncheon.

Then of a sudden she was seized by a vague dread of the unknown. She had closed the door behind her on entering, and as she stood alone in the long, silent, shadowy room, her dread seemed to take shape and sound, to be there audibly breathing and lurking among the shadows. Her short-sighted eyes strained through them, half-discerning an actual presence, something aloof, that watched and knew; and in the recoil from that intangible propinquity she threw herself suddenly on the bell-rope and gave it a desperate pull.

The long, quavering summons brought Trimmle in precipitately with a lamp, and Mary breathed again at this sobering reappearance of the usual.

"You may bring tea if Mr. Boyne is in," she said, to justify her ring.

"Very well, Madam. But Mr. Boyne is not in," said Trimmle, putting down the lamp.

"Not in? You mean he's come back and gone out again?"

"No, Madam. He's never been back."

The dread stirred again, and Mary knew that now it had her fast.

"Not since he went out with—the gentleman?"

"Not since he went out with the gentleman."

"But who WAS the gentleman?" Mary gasped out, with the sharp note of some one trying to be heard through a confusion of meaningless noises.

"That I couldn't say, Madam." Trimmle, standing there by the lamp, seemed suddenly to grow less round and rosy, as though eclipsed by the same creeping shade of apprehension.

"But the kitchen-maid knows—wasn't it the kitchen-maid who let him in?"

"She doesn't know either, Madam, for he wrote his name on a folded paper."

Mary, through her agitation, was aware that they were both designating the unknown visitor by a vague pronoun, instead of the conventional formula which, till then, had kept their allusions within the bounds of custom. And at the same moment her mind caught at the suggestion of the folded paper.

"But he must have a name! Where is the paper?"

She moved to the desk, and began to turn over the scattered documents that littered it. The first that caught her eye was an unfinished letter in her husband's hand, with his pen lying across it, as though dropped there at a sudden summons.

"My dear Parvis,"—who was Parvis?—"I have just received your letter announcing Elwell's death, and while I suppose there is now no farther risk of trouble, it might be safer—"

She tossed the sheet aside, and continued her search; but no folded paper was discoverable among the letters and pages of manuscript which had been swept together in a promiscuous heap, as if by a hurried or a startled gesture.

"But the kitchen-maid SAW him. Send her here," she commanded, wondering at her dullness in not thinking sooner of so simple a solution.

Trimmle, at the behest, vanished in a flash, as if thankful to be out of the room, and when she reappeared, conducting the agitated underling, Mary had regained her self-possession, and had her questions pat.

The gentleman was a stranger, yes—that she understood. But what had he said? And, above all, what had he looked like? The first question was easily enough answered, for the disconcerting reason that he had said so little—had merely asked for Mr. Boyne, and, scribbling something on a bit of paper, had requested that it should at once be carried in to him.

"Then you don't know what he wrote? You're not sure it WAS his name?"

The kitchen-maid was not sure, but supposed it was, since he had written it in answer to her inquiry as to whom she should announce.

"And when you carried the paper in to Mr. Boyne, what did he say?"

The kitchen-maid did not think that Mr. Boyne had said anything, but she could not be sure, for just as she had handed him the paper and he was opening it, she had become aware that the visitor had followed her into the library, and she had slipped out, leaving the two gentlemen together.

"But then, if you left them in the library, how do you know that they went out of the house?"

This question plunged the witness into momentary inarticulateness, from which she was rescued by Trimmle, who, by means of ingenious circumlocutions, elicited the statement that before she could cross the hall to the back passage she had heard the gentlemen behind her, and had seen them go out of the front door together.

"Then, if you saw the gentleman twice, you must be able to tell me what he looked like."

But with this final challenge to her powers of expression it became clear that the limit of the kitchen-maid's endurance had been reached. The obligation of going to the front door to "show in" a visitor was in itself so subversive of the fundamental order of things that it had thrown her faculties into hopeless disarray, and she could only stammer out, after various panting efforts at evocation, "His hat, mum, was different-like, as you might say—"

"Different? How different?" Mary flashed out at her, her own mind, in the same instant, leaping back to an image left on it that morning, but temporarily lost under layers of subsequent impressions.

"His hat had a wide brim, you mean? and his face was pale—a youngish face?" Mary pressed her, with a white-lipped intensity of interrogation. But if the kitchen-maid found any adequate answer to this challenge, it was swept away for her listener down the rushing current of her own convictions. The stranger—the stranger in the garden! Why had Mary not thought of him before? She needed no one now to tell her that it was he who had called for her husband and gone away with him. But who was he, and why had Boyne obeyed his call?

CHAPTER IV

It leaped out at her suddenly, like a grin out of the dark, that they had often called England so little—"such a confoundedly hard place to get lost in."

A CONFOUNDEDLY HARD PLACE TO GET LOST IN! That had been her husband's phrase. And now, with the whole machinery of official investigation sweeping its flash-lights from shore to shore, and across the dividing straits; now, with Boyne's name blazing from the walls of every town and village, his portrait (how that wrung her!) hawked up and down the country like the image of a hunted criminal; now the little compact, populous island, so policed, surveyed, and administered, revealed itself as a Sphinx-like guardian of abysmal mysteries, staring back into his wife's anguished eyes as if with the malicious joy of knowing something they would never know!

In the fortnight since Boyne's disappearance there had been no word of him, no trace of his movements. Even the usual misleading reports that raise expectancy in tortured bosoms had been few and fleeting. No one but the bewildered kitchen-maid had seen him leave the house, and no one else had seen "the gentleman" who accompanied him. All inquiries in the neighborhood failed to elicit the memory of a stranger's presence that day in the neighborhood of Lyng. And no one had met Edward Boyne, either alone or in company, in any of the neighboring villages, or on the road across the downs, or at either of the local railway-stations. The sunny English noon had swallowed him as completely as if he had gone out into Cimmerian night.

Mary, while every external means of investigation was working at its highest pressure, had ransacked her husband's papers for any trace of antecedent complications, of entanglements or obligations unknown to her, that might throw a faint ray into the darkness. But if any such had existed in the background of Boyne's life, they had disappeared as completely as the slip of paper on which the visitor had written his name. There remained no possible thread of guidance except—if it were indeed an exception—the letter which Boyne had apparently been in the act of writing when he received his mysterious summons. That letter, read and reread by his wife, and submitted by her to the police, yielded little enough for conjecture to feed on.

"I have just heard of Elwell's death, and while I suppose there is now no farther risk of trouble, it might be safer—" That was all. The "risk of trouble" was easily explained by the newspaper clipping which had apprised Mary of the suit brought against her husband by one of his associates in the Blue Star enterprise. The only new information conveyed in the letter was the fact of its showing Boyne, when he wrote it, to be still apprehensive of the results of the suit, though he had assured his wife that it had been withdrawn, and though the letter itself declared that the plaintiff was dead. It took several weeks of exhaustive cabling to fix the identity of the "Parvis" to whom the fragmentary communication was addressed, but even after these inquiries had shown him to be a Waukesha lawyer, no new facts concerning the Elwell suit were elicited. He appeared to have had no direct concern in it, but to have been conversant with the facts merely as an acquaintance, and possible intermediary; and he declared himself unable to divine with what object Boyne intended to seek his assistance.

This negative information, sole fruit of the first fortnight's feverish search, was not increased by a jot during the slow weeks that followed. Mary knew that the investigations were still being carried on, but she had a vague sense of their gradually slackening, as the actual march of time seemed to slacken. It was as though the days, flying horror-struck from the shrouded image of the one inscrutable day, gained assurance as the distance lengthened, till at last they fell back into their normal gait. And so with the human imaginations at work on the dark event. No doubt it occupied them still, but week by week and hour by hour it grew less absorbing, took up less space, was slowly but inevitably crowded out of the foreground of consciousness by the new problems perpetually bubbling up from the vaporous caldron of human experience.

Even Mary Boyne's consciousness gradually felt

the same lowering of velocity. It still swayed with the incessant oscillations of conjecture; but they were slower, more rhythmical in their beat. There were moments of overwhelming lassitude when, like the victim of some poison which leaves the brain clear, but holds the body motionless, she saw herself domesticated with the Horror, accepting its perpetual presence as one of the fixed conditions of life.

These moments lengthened into hours and days, till she passed into a phase of stolid acquiescence. She watched the familiar routine of life with the incurious eye of a savage on whom the meaningless processes of civilization make but the faintest impression. She had come to regard herself as part of the routine, a spoke of the wheel, revolving with its motion; she felt almost like the furniture of the room in which she sat, an insensate object to be dusted and pushed about with the chairs and tables. And this deepening apathy held her fast at Lyng, in spite of the urgent entreaties of friends and the usual medical recommendation of "change." Her friends supposed that her refusal to move was inspired by the belief that her husband would one day return to the spot from which he had vanished, and a beautiful legend grew up about this imaginary state of waiting. But in reality she had no such belief: the depths of anguish inclosing her were no longer lighted by flashes of hope. She was sure that Boyne would never come back, that he had gone out of her sight as completely as if Death itself had waited that day on the threshold. She had even renounced, one by one, the various theories as to his disappearance which had been advanced by the press, the police, and her own agonized imagination. In sheer lassitude her mind turned from these alternatives of horror, and sank back into the blank fact that he was gone.

No, she would never know what had become of him—no one would ever know. But the house KNEW; the library in which she spent her long, lonely evenings knew. For it was here that the last scene had been enacted, here that the stranger had come, and spoken the word which had caused Boyne to rise and follow him. The floor she trod had felt his tread; the books on the shelves had seen his face; and there were moments when the intense consciousness of the old, dusky walls seemed about to break out into some audible revelation of their secret. But the revelation never came, and she knew it would never come. Lyng was not one of the garrulous old houses that betray the secrets intrusted to them. Its very legend proved that it had always been the mute accomplice, the incorruptible custodian of the mysteries it had surprised. And Mary Boyne, sitting face to face with its portentous silence, felt the futility of seeking to break it by any human means.

CHAPTER V

"I don't say it WASN'T straight, yet don't say it WAS straight. It was business."

Mary, at the words, lifted her head with a start, and looked intently at the speaker.

When, half an hour before, a card with "Mr. Parvis" on it had been brought up to her, she had been immediately aware that the name had been a part of her consciousness ever since she had read it at the head of Boyne's unfinished letter. In the library she had found awaiting her a small neutral-tinted man with a bald head and gold eye-glasses, and it sent a strange tremor through her to know that this was the person to whom her husband's last known thought had been directed.

Parvis, civilly, but without vain preamble,—in the manner of a man who has his watch in his hand,—had set forth the object of his visit. He had "run over" to England on business, and finding himself in the neighborhood of Dorchester, had not wished to leave it without paying his respects to Mrs. Boyne; without asking her, if the occasion offered, what she meant to do about Bob Elwell's family.

The words touched the spring of some obscure dread in Mary's bosom. Did her visitor, after all, know what Boyne had meant by his unfinished phrase? She asked for an elucidation of his question, and noticed at once that he seemed surprised at her continued ignorance of the subject. Was it possible that she really knew as little as she said?

"I know nothing—you must tell me," she faltered out; and her visitor thereupon proceeded to unfold his story. It threw, even to her confused perceptions, and imperfectly initiated vision, a lurid glare on the whole hazy episode of the Blue Star Mine. Her husband had made his money in that brilliant speculation at the cost of "getting ahead" of some one less alert to seize the chance; the victim of his ingenuity was young Robert Elwell, who had "put him on" to the Blue Star scheme.

Parvis, at Mary's first startled cry, had thrown her a sobering glance through his impartial glasses.

"Bob Elwell wasn't smart enough, that's all; if he had been, he might have turned round and served Boyne the same way. It's the kind of thing that happens every day in business. I guess it's what the scientists call the survival of the fittest," said Mr. Parvis, evidently pleased with the aptness of his analogy.

Mary felt a physical shrinking from the next question she tried to frame; it was as though the words on her lips had a taste that nauseated her.

"But then—you accuse my husband of doing something dishonorable?"

Mr. Parvis surveyed the question dispassionately. "Oh, no,

I don't. I don't even say it wasn't straight." He glanced up and down the long lines of books, as if one of them might have supplied him with the definition he sought. "I don't say it WASN'T straight, and yet I don't say it WAS straight. It was business." After all, no definition in his category could be more comprehensive than that.

Mary sat staring at him with a look of terror. He seemed to her like the indifferent, implacable emissary of some dark, formless power.

"But Mr. Elwell's lawyers apparently did not take your view, since I suppose the suit was withdrawn by their advice."

"Oh, yes, they knew he hadn't a leg to stand on, technically. It was when they advised him to withdraw the suit that he got desperate. You see, he'd borrowed most of the money he lost in the Blue Star, and he was up a tree. That's why he shot himself when they told him he had no show."

The horror was sweeping over Mary in great, deafening waves.

"He shot himself? He killed himself because of THAT?"

"Well, he didn't kill himself, exactly. He dragged on two months before he died." Parvis emitted the statement as unemotionally as a gramophone grinding out its "record."

"You mean that he tried to kill himself, and failed? And tried again?"

"Oh, he didn't have to try again," said Parvis, grimly.

They sat opposite each other in silence, he swinging his eyeglass thoughtfully about his finger, she, motionless, her arms stretched along her knees in an attitude of rigid tension.

"But if you knew all this," she began at length, hardly able to force her voice above a whisper, "how is it that when I wrote you at the time of my husband's disappearance you said you didn't understand his letter?"

Parvis received this without perceptible discomfiture. "Why, I didn't understand it—strictly speaking. And it wasn't the time to talk about it, if I had. The Elwell business was settled when the suit was withdrawn. Nothing I could have told you would have helped you to find your husband."

Mary continued to scrutinize him. "Then why are you telling me now?"

Still Parvis did not hesitate. "Well, to begin with, I supposed you knew more than you appear to—I mean about the circumstances of Elwell's death. And then people are talking of it now; the whole matter's been raked up again. And I thought, if you didn't know, you ought to."

She remained silent, and he continued: "You see, it's only come out lately what a bad state Elwell's affairs were in. His wife's a proud woman, and she fought on as long as she could, going out to work, and taking sewing at home, when she got too sick—something with the heart, I believe. But she had his bedridden mother to look after, and the children, and she broke down under it, and finally had to ask for help. That attracted attention to the case, and the papers took it up, and a subscription was started. Everybody out there liked Bob Elwell, and most of the prominent names in the place are down on the list, and people began to wonder why—"

Parvis broke off to fumble in an inner pocket. "Here," he continued, "here's an account of the whole thing from the 'Sentinel'—a little sensational, of course. But I guess you'd better look it over."

He held out a newspaper to Mary, who unfolded it slowly, remembering, as she did so, the evening when, in that same room, the perusal of a clipping from the "Sentinel" had first shaken the depths of her security.

As she opened the paper, her eyes, shrinking from the glaring head-lines, "Widow of Boyne's Victim Forced to Appeal for Aid," ran down the column of text to two portraits inserted in it. The first was her husband's, taken from a photograph made the year they had come to England. It was the picture of him that she liked best, the one that stood on the writing-table up-stairs in her bedroom. As the eyes in the photograph met hers, she felt it would be impossible to read what was said of him, and closed her lids with the sharpness of the pain.

"I thought if you felt disposed to put your name down—" she heard Parvis continue.

She opened her eyes with an effort, and they fell on the other portrait. It was that of a youngish man, slightly built, in rough clothes, with features somewhat blurred by the shadow of a projecting hat-brim. Where had she seen that outline before? She stared at it confusedly, her heart hammering in her throat and ears. Then she gave a cry.

"This is the man—the man who came for my husband!"

She heard Parvis start to his feet, and was dimly aware that she had slipped backward into the corner of the sofa, and that he was bending above her in alarm. With an intense effort she straightened herself, and reached out for the paper, which she had dropped.

"It's the man! I should know him anywhere!" she cried in a voice that sounded in her own ears like a scream.

Parvis's voice seemed to come to her from far off, down endless, fog-muffled windings.

"Mrs. Boyne, you're not very well. Shall I call somebody? Shall I get a glass of water?"

"No, no, no!" She threw herself toward him, her hand frantically clenching the newspaper. "I tell you, it's the man! I KNOW him! He spoke to me in the garden!"

Parvis took the journal from her, directing his glasses to the portrait. "It can't be, Mrs. Boyne. It's Robert Elwell."

"Robert Elwell?" Her white stare seemed to travel into space. "Then it was Robert Elwell who came for him."

"Came for Boyne? The day he went away?" Parvis's voice dropped as hers rose. He bent over, laying a fraternal hand on her, as if to coax her gently back into her seat. "Why, Elwell was dead! Don't you remember?"

Mary sat with her eyes fixed on the picture, unconscious of what he was saying.

"Don't you remember Boyne's unfinished letter to me— the one you found on his desk that day? It was written just after he'd heard of Elwell's death." She noticed an odd shake in Parvis's unemotional voice. "Surely you remember that!" he urged her.

Yes, she remembered: that was the profoundest horror of it. Elwell had died the day before her husband's disappearance; and this was Elwell's portrait; and it was the portrait of the man who had spoken to her in the garden. She lifted her head and looked slowly about the library. The library could have borne witness that it was also the portrait of the man who had come in that day to call Boyne from his unfinished letter. Through the misty surgings of her brain she heard the faint boom of half-forgotten words—words spoken by Alida Stair on the lawn at Pangbourne before Boyne and his wife had ever seen the house at Lyng, or had imagined that they might one day live there.

"This was the man who spoke to me," she repeated.

She looked again at Parvis. He was trying to conceal his disturbance under what he imagined to be an expression of indulgent commiseration; but the edges of his lips were blue. "He thinks me mad; but I'm not mad," she reflected; and suddenly there flashed upon her a way of justifying her strange affirmation.

She sat quiet, controlling the quiver of her lips, and waiting till she could trust her voice to keep its habitual level; then she said, looking straight at Parvis: "Will you answer me one question, please? When was it that Robert Elwell tried to kill himself?"

"When—when?" Parvis stammered.

"Yes; the date. Please try to remember."

She saw that he was growing still more afraid of her. "I have a reason," she insisted gently.

"Yes, yes. Only I can't remember. About two months before, I should say."

"I want the date," she repeated.

Parvis picked up the newspaper. "We might see here," he said, still humoring her. He ran his eyes down the page. "Here it is. Last October—the—"

She caught the words from him. "The 20th, wasn't it?" With a sharp look at her, he verified. "Yes, the 20th. Then you DID know?"

"I know now." Her white stare continued to travel past him. "Sunday, the 20th—that was the day he came first."

Parvis's voice was almost inaudible. "Came HERE first?"

"Yes."

"You saw him twice, then?"

"Yes, twice." She breathed it at him with dilated eyes. "He came first on the 20th of October. I remember the date because it was the day we went up Meldon Steep for the first time." She felt a faint gasp of inward laughter at the thought that but for that she might have forgotten.

Parvis continued to scrutinize her, as if trying to intercept her gaze.

"We saw him from the roof," she went on. "He came down the lime-avenue toward the house. He was dressed just as he is in that picture. My husband saw him first. He was frightened, and ran down ahead of me; but there was no one there. He had vanished."

"Elwell had vanished?" Parvis faltered.

"Yes." Their two whispers seemed to grope for each other. "I couldn't think what had happened. I see now. He TRIED to come then; but he wasn't dead enough—he couldn't reach us. He had to wait for two months; and then he came back again—and Ned went with him."

She nodded at Parvis with the look of triumph of a child who has successfully worked out a difficult puzzle. But suddenly she lifted her hands with a desperate gesture, pressing them to her bursting temples.

"Oh, my God! I sent him to Ned—I told him where to go! I sent him to this room!" she screamed out.

She felt the walls of the room rush toward her, like inward falling ruins; and she heard Parvis, a long way off, as if through the ruins, crying to her, and struggling to get at her. But she was numb to his touch, she did not know what he was saying. Through the tumult she heard but one clear note, the voice of Alida Stair, speaking on the lawn at Pangbourne.

"You won't know till afterward," it said. "You won't know till long, long afterward."

THE END OF AFTERWARD

THE FULNESS OF LIFE

December 1893

CHAPTER I

For hours she had lain in a kind of gentle torpor, not
unlike that sweet lassitude which masters one in the hush of
a midsummer noon, when the heat seems to have silenced
the very birds and insects, and, lying sunk in the tasselled
meadow-grasses, one looks up through a level roofing of
maple-leaves at the vast shadowless, and unsuggestive blue.
Now and then, at ever-lengthening intervals, a flash of pain
darted through her, like the ripple of sheet-lightning across
such a midsummer sky; but it was too transitory to shake her
stupor, that calm, delicious, bottomless stupor into which
she felt herself sinking more and more deeply, without a
disturbing impulse of resistance, an effort of reattachment
to the vanishing edges of consciousness.

The resistance, the effort, had known their hour of
violence; but now they were at an end. Through her mind,
long harried by grotesque visions, fragmentary images of the
life that she was leaving, tormenting lines of verse, obstinate
presentments of pictures once beheld, indistinct impressions
of rivers, towers, and cupolas, gathered in the length of
journeys half forgotten—through her mind there now only

moved a few primal sensations of colorless well-being; a vague satisfaction in the thought that she had swallowed her noxious last draught of medicine... and that she should never again hear the creaking of her husband's boots—those horrible boots—and that no one would come to bother her about the next day's dinner... or the butcher's book....

At last even these dim sensations spent themselves in the thickening obscurity which enveloped her; a dusk now filled with pale geometric roses, circling softly, interminably before her, now darkened to a uniform blue-blackness, the hue of a summer night without stars. And into this darkness she felt herself sinking, sinking, with the gentle sense of security of one upheld from beneath. Like a tepid tide it rose around her, gliding ever higher and higher, folding in its velvety embrace her relaxed and tired body, now submerging her breast and shoulders, now creeping gradually, with soft inexorableness, over her throat to her chin, to her ears, to her mouth.... Ah, now it was rising too high; the impulse to struggle was renewed;... her mouth was full;... she was choking.... Help!

"It is all over," said the nurse, drawing down the eyelids with official composure.

The clock struck three. They remembered it afterward. Someone opened the window and let in a blast of that strange, neutral air which walks the earth between darkness and dawn; someone else led the husband into another room.

He walked vaguely, like a blind man, on his creaking boots.

CHAPTER II

She stood, as it seemed, on a threshold, yet no tangible gateway was in front of her. Only a wide vista of light, mild yet penetrating as the gathered glimmer of innumerable stars, expanded gradually before her eyes, in blissful contrast to the cavernous darkness from which she had of late emerged.

She stepped forward, not frightened, but hesitating, and as her eyes began to grow more familiar with the melting depths of light about her, she distinguished the outlines of a landscape, at first swimming in the opaline uncertainty of Shelley's vaporous creations, then gradually resolved into distincter shape—the vast unrolling of a sunlit plain, aerial forms of mountains, and presently the silver crescent of a river in the valley, and a blue stencilling of trees along its curve—something suggestive in its ineffable hue of an azure background of Leonardo's, strange, enchanting, mysterious, leading on the eye and the imagination into regions of fabulous delight. As she gazed, her heart beat with a soft and rapturous surprise; so exquisite a promise she read in the summons of that hyaline distance.

"And so death is not the end after all," in sheer gladness she heard herself exclaiming aloud. "I always knew that it couldn't be. I believed in Darwin, of course. I do still; but then Darwin himself said that he wasn't sure about the soul—at least, I think he did—and Wallace was a spiritualist;

and then there was St. George Mivart—"

Her gaze lost itself in the ethereal remoteness of the mountains.

"How beautiful! How satisfying!" she murmured. "Perhaps now I shall really know what it is to live."

As she spoke she felt a sudden thickening of her heartbeats, and looking up she was aware that before her stood the Spirit of Life.

"Have you never really known what it is to live?" the Spirit of Life asked her.

"I have never known," she replied, "that fulness of life which we all feel ourselves capable of knowing; though my life has not been without scattered hints of it, like the scent of earth which comes to one sometimes far out at sea."

"And what do you call the fulness of life?" the Spirit asked again.

"Oh, I can't tell you, if you don't know," she said, almost reproachfully. "Many words are supposed to define it—love and sympathy are those in commonest use, but I am not even sure that they are the right ones, and so few people really know what they mean."

"You were married," said the Spirit, "yet you did not find the fulness of life in your marriage?"

"Oh, dear, no," she replied, with an indulgent scorn, "my marriage was a very incomplete affair."

"And yet you were fond of your husband?"

"You have hit upon the exact word; I was fond of him, yes, just as I was fond of my grandmother, and the house that I was born in, and my old nurse. Oh, I was fond of him, and we were counted a very happy couple. But I have sometimes thought that a woman's nature is like a great house full of rooms: there is the hall, through which everyone passes in going in and out; the drawing-room, where one receives formal visits; the sitting-room, where the members of the family come and go as they list; but beyond that, far beyond, are other rooms, the handles of whose doors perhaps are never turned; no one knows the way to them, no one knows whither they lead; and in the innermost room, the holy of holies, the soul sits alone and waits for a footstep that never comes."

"And your husband," asked the Spirit, after a pause, "never got beyond the family sitting-room?"

"Never," she returned, impatiently; "and the worst of it was that he was quite content to remain there. He thought it perfectly beautiful, and sometimes, when he was admiring its commonplace furniture, insignificant as the chairs and tables of a hotel parlor, I felt like crying out to him: 'Fool, will you never guess that close at hand are rooms full of treasures and wonders, such as the eye of man hath not seen, rooms that no step has crossed, but that might be yours to live in, could you but find the handle of the door?'"

"Then," the Spirit continued, "those moments of which

you lately spoke, which seemed to come to you like scattered hints of the fulness of life, were not shared with your husband?"

"Oh, no—never. He was different. His boots creaked, and he always slammed the door when he went out, and he never read anything but railway novels and the sporting advertisements in the papers—and—and, in short, we never understood each other in the least."

"To what influence, then, did you owe those exquisite sensations?"

"I can hardly tell. Sometimes to the perfume of a flower; sometimes to a verse of Dante or of Shakespeare; sometimes to a picture or a sunset, or to one of those calm days at sea, when one seems to be lying in the hollow of a blue pearl; sometimes, but rarely, to a word spoken by someone who chanced to give utterance, at the right moment, to what I felt but could not express."

"Someone whom you loved?" asked the Spirit.

"I never loved anyone, in that way," she said, rather sadly, "nor was I thinking of any one person when I spoke, but of two or three who, by touching for an instant upon a certain chord of my being, had called forth a single note of that strange melody which seemed sleeping in my soul. It has seldom happened, however, that I have owed such feelings to people; and no one ever gave me a moment of such happiness as it was my lot to feel one evening in the Church of Or San Michele, in Florence."

"Tell me about it," said the Spirit.

"It was near sunset on a rainy spring afternoon in Easter week. The clouds had vanished, dispersed by a sudden wind, and as we entered the church the fiery panes of the high windows shone out like lamps through the dusk. A priest was at the high altar, his white cope a livid spot in the incense-laden obscurity, the light of the candles flickering up and down like fireflies about his head; a few people knelt near by. We stole behind them and sat down on a bench close to the tabernacle of Orcagna.

"Strange to say, though Florence was not new to me, I had never been in the church before; and in that magical light I saw for the first time the inlaid steps, the fluted columns, the sculptured bas-reliefs and canopy of the marvellous shrine. The marble, worn and mellowed by the subtle hand of time, took on an unspeakable rosy hue, suggestive in some remote way of the honey-colored columns of the Parthenon, but more mystic, more complex, a color not born of the sun's inveterate kiss, but made up of cryptal twilight, and the flame of candles upon martyrs' tombs, and gleams of sunset through symbolic panes of chrysoprase and ruby; such a light as illumines the missals in the library of Siena, or burns like a hidden fire through the Madonna of Gian Bellini in the Church of the Redeemer, at Venice; the light of the Middle Ages, richer, more solemn, more significant than the limpid sunshine of Greece.

"The church was silent, but for the wail of the priest and the occasional scraping of a chair against the floor, and as I sat there, bathed in that light, absorbed in rapt contemplation of the marble miracle which rose before me, cunningly wrought as a casket of ivory and enriched with jewel-like incrustations and tarnished gleams of gold, I felt myself borne onward along a mighty current, whose source seemed to be in the very beginning of things, and whose tremendous waters gathered as they went all the mingled streams of human passion and endeavor. Life in all its varied manifestations of beauty and strangeness seemed weaving a rhythmical dance around me as I moved, and wherever the spirit of man had passed I knew that my foot had once been familiar.

"As I gazed the mediaeval bosses of the tabernacle of Orcagna seemed to melt and flow into their primal forms so that the folded lotus of the Nile and the Greek acanthus were braided with the runic knots and fish-tailed monsters of the North, and all the plastic terror and beauty born of man's hand from the Ganges to the Baltic quivered and mingled in Orcagna's apotheosis of Mary. And so the river bore me on, past the alien face of antique civilizations and the familiar wonders of Greece, till I swam upon the fiercely rushing tide of the Middle Ages, with its swirling eddies of passion, its heaven-reflecting pools of poetry and art; I heard the rhythmic blow of the craftsmen's hammers in the goldsmiths' workshops and on the walls of churches, the party-cries of armed factions in the narrow streets, the organ-roll of Dante's verse, the crackle of the fagots around Arnold of Brescia, the twitter of the swallows to which St. Francis preached, the laughter of the ladies listening on the hillside to the quips of the Decameron, while plague-struck Florence howled beneath them—all this and much more I heard, joined in strange unison with voices earlier and more remote, fierce, passionate, or tender, yet subdued to such awful harmony that I thought of the song that the morning stars sang together and felt as though it were sounding in my ears. My heart beat to suffocation, the tears burned my lids, the joy, the mystery of it seemed too intolerable to be borne. I could not understand even then the words of the song; but I knew that if there had been someone at my side who could have heard it with me, we might have found the key to it together.

"I turned to my husband, who was sitting beside me in an attitude of patient dejection, gazing into the bottom of his hat; but at that moment he rose, and stretching his stiffened legs, said, mildly: 'Hadn't we better be going? There doesn't seem to be much to see here, and you know the table d'hote dinner is at half-past six o'clock."

Her recital ended, there was an interval of silence; then the Spirit of Life said: "There is a compensation in store for such needs as you have expressed."

"Oh, then you DO understand?" she exclaimed. "Tell me what compensation, I entreat you!"

"It is ordained," the Spirit answered, "that every soul which seeks in vain on earth for a kindred soul to whom it can lay bare its inmost being shall find that soul here and be united to it for eternity."

A glad cry broke from her lips. "Ah, shall I find him at last?" she cried, exultant.

"He is here," said the Spirit of Life.

She looked up and saw that a man stood near whose soul (for in that unwonted light she seemed to see his soul more clearly than his face) drew her toward him with an invincible force.

"Are you really he?" she murmured.

"I am he," he answered.

She laid her hand in his and drew him toward the parapet which overhung the valley.

"Shall we go down together," she asked him, "into that marvellous country; shall we see it together, as if with the self-same eyes, and tell each other in the same words all that we think and feel?"

"So," he replied, "have I hoped and dreamed."

"What?" she asked, with rising joy. "Then you, too, have looked for me?"

"All my life."

"How wonderful! And did you never, never find anyone in the other world who understood you?"

"Not wholly—not as you and I understand each other."

"Then you feel it, too? Oh, I am happy," she sighed.

They stood, hand in hand, looking down over the parapet upon the shimmering landscape which stretched forth beneath them into sapphirine space, and the Spirit of Life, who kept watch near the threshold, heard now and then a floating fragment of their talk blown backward like the stray swallows which the wind sometimes separates from their migratory tribe.

"Did you never feel at sunset—"

"Ah, yes; but I never heard anyone else say so. Did you?"

"Do you remember that line in the third canto of the 'Inferno?'"

"Ah, that line—my favorite always. Is it possible—"

"You know the stooping Victory in the frieze of the Nike Apteros?"

"You mean the one who is tying her sandal? Then you have noticed, too, that all Botticelli and Mantegna are dormant in those flying folds of her drapery?"

"After a storm in autumn have you never seen—"

"Yes, it is curious how certain flowers suggest certain painters—the perfume of the incarnation, Leonardo; that of the rose, Titian; the tuberose, Crivelli—"

"I never supposed that anyone else had noticed it."

"Have you never thought—"

"Oh, yes, often and often; but I never dreamed that anyone else had."

"But surely you must have felt—"

"Oh, yes, yes; and you, too—"

"How beautiful! How strange—"

Their voices rose and fell, like the murmur of two fountains answering each other across a garden full of flowers. At length, with a certain tender impatience, he turned to her and said: "Love, why should we linger here? All eternity lies before us. Let us go down into that beautiful country together and make a home for ourselves on some blue hill above the shining river."

As he spoke, the hand she had forgotten in his was suddenly withdrawn, and he felt that a cloud was passing over the radiance of her soul.

"A home," she repeated, slowly, "a home for you and me to live in for all eternity?"

"Why not, love? Am I not the soul that yours has sought?"

"Y-yes—yes, I know—but, don't you see, home would not be like home to me, unless—"

"Unless?" he wonderingly repeated.

She did not answer, but she thought to herself, with an impulse of whimsical inconsistency, "Unless you slammed the door and wore creaking boots."

But he had recovered his hold upon her hand, and by imperceptible degrees was leading her toward the shining steps which descended to the valley.

"Come, O my soul's soul," he passionately implored; "why delay a moment? Surely you feel, as I do, that eternity itself is too short to hold such bliss as ours. It seems to me that I can see our home already. Have I not always seem it in my dreams? It is white, love, is it not, with polished columns, and a sculptured cornice against the blue? Groves of laurel and oleander and thickets of roses surround it; but from the terrace where we walk at sunset, the eye looks out over woodlands and cool meadows where, deep-bowered under ancient boughs, a stream goes delicately toward the river. Indoors our favorite pictures hang upon the walls and the rooms are lined with books. Think, dear, at last we shall have time to read them all. With which shall we begin? Come, help me to choose. Shall it be 'Faust' or the 'Vita Nuova,' the 'Tempest' or 'Les Caprices de Marianne,' or the thirty-first canto of the 'Paradise,' or 'Epipsychidion' or 'Lycidas'? Tell me, dear, which one?"

As he spoke he saw the answer trembling joyously upon her lips; but it died in the ensuing silence, and she stood motionless, resisting the persuasion of his hand.

"What is it?" he entreated.

"Wait a moment," she said, with a strange hesitation in her voice. "Tell me first, are you quite sure of yourself? Is there

71

no one on earth whom you sometimes remember?"

"Not since I have seen you," he replied; for, being a man, he had indeed forgotten.

Still she stood motionless, and he saw that the shadow deepened on her soul.

"Surely, love," he rebuked her, "it was not that which troubled you? For my part I have walked through Lethe. The past has melted like a cloud before the moon. I never lived until I saw you."

She made no answer to his pleadings, but at length, rousing herself with a visible effort, she turned away from him and moved toward the Spirit of Life, who still stood near the threshold.

"I want to ask you a question," she said, in a troubled voice.

"Ask," said the Spirit.

"A little while ago," she began, slowly, "you told me that every soul which has not found a kindred soul on earth is destined to find one here."

"And have you not found one?" asked the Spirit.

"Yes; but will it be so with my husband's soul also?"

"No," answered the Spirit of Life, "for your husband imagined that he had found his soul's mate on earth in you; and for such delusions eternity itself contains no cure."

She gave a little cry. Was it of disappointment or triumph?

"Then—then what will happen to him when he comes here?"

"That I cannot tell you. Some field of activity and happiness he will doubtless find, in due measure to his capacity for being active and happy."

She interrupted, almost angrily: "He will never be happy without me."

"Do not be too sure of that," said the Spirit.

She took no notice of this, and the Spirit continued: "He will not understand you here any better than he did on earth."

"No matter," she said; "I shall be the only sufferer, for he always thought that he understood me."

"His boots will creak just as much as ever—"

"No matter."

"And he will slam the door—"

"Very likely."

"And continue to read railway novels—"

She interposed, impatiently: "Many men do worse than that."

"But you said just now," said the Spirit, "that you did not love him."

"True," she answered, simply; "but don't you understand that I shouldn't feel at home without him? It is all very well for a week or two—but for eternity! After all, I never minded the creaking of his boots, except when my head ached, and I don't suppose it will ache HERE; and he was always so sorry when he had slammed the door, only he never COULD remember not to. Besides, no one else would know how to look after him, he is so helpless. His inkstand would never be filled, and he would always be out of stamps and visiting-cards. He would never remember to have his umbrella recovered, or to ask the price of anything before he bought it. Why, he wouldn't even know what novels to read. I always had to choose the kind he liked, with a murder or a forgery and a successful detective."

She turned abruptly to her kindred soul, who stood listening with a mien of wonder and dismay.

"Don't you see," she said, "that I can't possibly go with you?"

"But what do you intend to do?" asked the Spirit of Life.

"What do I intend to do?" she returned, indignantly. "Why, I mean to wait for my husband, of course. If he had come here first HE would have waited for me for years and years; and it would break his heart not to find me here when he comes." She pointed with a contemptuous gesture to the magic vision of hill and vale sloping away to the translucent mountains. "He wouldn't give a fig for all that," she said, "if he didn't find me here."

"But consider," warned the Spirit, "that you are now choosing for eternity. It is a solemn moment."

"Choosing!" she said, with a half-sad smile. "Do you still

keep up here that old fiction about choosing? I should have thought that YOU knew better than that. How can I help myself? He will expect to find me here when he comes, and he would never believe you if you told him that I had gone away with someone else—never, never."

"So be it," said the Spirit. "Here, as on earth, each one must decide for himself."

She turned to her kindred soul and looked at him gently, almost wistfully. "I am sorry," she said. "I should have liked to talk with you again; but you will understand, I know, and I dare say you will find someone else a great deal cleverer—"

And without pausing to hear his answer she waved him a swift farewell and turned back toward the threshold.

"Will my husband come soon?" she asked the Spirit of Life.

"That you are not destined to know," the Spirit replied.

"No matter," she said, cheerfully; "I have all eternity to wait in."

And still seated alone on the threshold, she listens for the creaking of his boots.

THE END OF THE FULNESS OF LIFE

A VENETIAN NIGHT'S ENTERTAINMENT

December 1903

This is the story that, in the dining-room of the old Beacon Street house (now the Aldebaran Club), Judge Anthony Bracknell, of the famous East India firm of Bracknell & Saulsbee, when the ladies had withdrawn to the oval parlour (and Maria's harp was throwing its gauzy web of sound across the Common), used to relate to his grandsons, about the year that Buonaparte marched upon Moscow.

CHAPTER I

"Him Venice!" said the Lascar with the big earrings; and Tony Bracknell, leaning on the high gunwale of his father's East Indiaman, the Hepzibah B., saw far off, across the morning sea, a faint vision of towers and domes dissolved in golden air.

It was a rare February day of the year 1760, and a young Tony, newly of age, and bound on the grand tour aboard the crack merchantman of old Bracknell's fleet, felt his heart leap up as the distant city trembled into shape. VENICE! The name, since childhood, had been a magician's wand to him. In the hall of the old Bracknell house at Salem there hung a series of yellowing prints which Uncle Richard Saulsbee had brought home from one of his long voyages: views of heathen mosques and palaces, of the Grand Turk's Seraglio, of St. Peter's Church in Rome; and, in a corner—the corner nearest the rack where the old flintlocks hung—a busy merry populous scene, entitled: ST. MARK'S SQUARE IN VENICE. This picture, from the first, had singularly taken little Tony's fancy. His unformulated criticism on the others was that they lacked action. True, in the view of St. Peter's an experienced-looking gentleman in a full-bottomed wig was pointing out the fairly obvious monument to a bashful companion, who had presumably not ventured to raise his eyes to it; while, at the doors of the Seraglio, a group of turbaned infidels observed with less hesitancy the approach of a veiled lady on a camel. But in Venice so many things were happening at once—more, Tony was sure, than had ever happened in Boston in a twelve-month or in Salem in a long lifetime. For here, by their garb, were people of every nation on earth, Chinamen, Turks, Spaniards, and many more, mixed with a parti-coloured throng of gentry, lacqueys, chapmen, hucksters, and tall personages in parsons' gowns who stalked through the crowd with an air of mastery, a string of parasites at their heels. And all these people seemed to be diverting themselves hugely, chaffering with the hucksters, watching the antics of trained dogs and monkeys, distributing doles to maimed beggars or having their pockets picked by slippery-looking fellows in black— the whole with such an air of ease and good-humour that one felt the cut-purses to be as much a part of the show as the tumbling acrobats and animals.

As Tony advanced in years and experience this childish mumming lost its magic; but not so the early imaginings it had excited. For the old picture had been but the spring-board of fancy, the first step of a cloud-ladder leading to a land of dreams. With these dreams the name of Venice remained associated; and all that observation or report subsequently brought him concerning the place seemed, on a sober warranty of fact, to confirm its claim to stand midway between reality and illusion. There was, for instance, a slender Venice glass, gold-powdered as with lily-pollen or the dust of sunbeams, that, standing in the corner cabinet betwixt two Lowestoft caddies, seemed, among its lifeless neighbours, to palpitate like an impaled butterfly. There was, farther, a gold chain of his mother's, spun of that same sun-pollen, so thread-like, impalpable, that it slipped through the fingers like light, yet so strong that it carried a heavy pendant which seemed held in air as if by magic. MAGIC! That was the word which the thought of Venice evoked. It was the kind of place, Tony felt, in which things elsewhere impossible might naturally happen, in which two and two might make five, a paradox elope with a syllogism, and a conclusion give the lie to its own premiss. Was there ever a young heart that did not, once and again, long to get away into such a world as that? Tony, at least, had felt the longing from the first hour when the axioms in his horn-book had brought home to him his heavy responsibilities as a Christian and a sinner. And now here was his wish taking shape before him, as the distant haze of gold shaped itself into towers and domes across the morning sea!

The Reverend Ozias Mounce, Tony's governor and bear-leader, was just putting a hand to the third clause of the fourth part of a sermon on Free-Will and Predestination as the Hepzibah B.'s anchor rattled overboard. Tony, in his haste to be ashore, would have made one plunge with the anchor; but the Reverend Ozias, on being roused from his lucubrations, earnestly protested against leaving his argument in suspense. What was the trifle of an arrival at some Papistical foreign city, where the very churches wore turbans like so many Moslem idolators, to the important fact of Mr. Mounce's summing up his conclusions before the Muse of Theology took flight? He should be happy, he said, if the tide served, to visit Venice with Mr. Bracknell the next morning.

The next morning, ha!—Tony murmured a submissive "Yes, sir," winked at the subjugated captain, buckled on his sword, pressed his hat down with a flourish, and before the Reverend Ozias had arrived at his next deduction, was skimming merrily shoreward in the Hepzibah's gig.

A moment more and he was in the thick of it! Here was the very world of the old print, only suffused with sunlight and colour, and bubbling with merry noises. What a scene it was! A square enclosed in fantastic painted buildings, and peopled with a throng as fantastic: a bawling, laughing, jostling, sweating mob, parti-coloured, parti-speeched, crackling and sputtering under the hot sun like a dish of fritters over a kitchen fire. Tony, agape, shouldered his way through the press, aware at once that, spite of the tumult, the shrillness, the gesticulation, there was no undercurrent of clownishness, no tendency to horse-play, as in such crowds on market-day at home, but a kind of facetious suavity which seemed to include everybody in the circumference of one huge joke.

In such an air the sense of strangeness soon wore off, and Tony was beginning to feel himself vastly at home, when a lift of the tide bore him against a droll-looking bell-ringing fellow who carried above his head a tall metal tree hung with sherbet-glasses.

The encounter set the glasses spinning and three or four spun off and clattered to the stones. The sherbet-seller called on all the saints, and Tony, clapping a lordly hand to his pocket, tossed him a ducat by mistake for a sequin. The fellow's eyes shot out of their orbits, and just then a personable-looking young man who had observed the transaction stepped up to Tony and said pleasantly, in English:

"I perceive, sir, that you are not familiar with our currency."

"Does he want more?" says Tony, very lordly; whereat the other laughed and replied: "You have given him enough to retire from his business and open a gaming-house over the arcade."

Tony joined in the laugh, and this incident bridging the preliminaries, the two young men were presently hobnobbing over a glass of Canary in front of one of the coffee-houses about the square. Tony counted himself lucky to have run across an English-speaking companion who was good-natured enough to give him a clue to the labyrinth; and when he had paid for the Canary (in the coin his friend selected) they set out again to view the town. The Italian gentleman, who called himself Count Rialto, appeared to have a very numerous acquaintance, and was able to point out to Tony all the chief dignitaries of the state, the men of ton and ladies of fashion, as well as a number of other characters of a kind not openly mentioned in taking a census of Salem.

Tony, who was not averse from reading when nothing better offered, had perused the "Merchant of Venice" and Mr. Otway's fine tragedy; but though these pieces had given him a notion that the social usages of Venice differed from those at home, he was unprepared for the surprising appearance and manners of the great people his friend named to him. The gravest Senators of the Republic went in prodigious striped trousers, short cloaks and feathered hats. One nobleman wore a ruff and doctor's gown, another a black velvet tunic slashed with rose-colour; while the President of the dreaded Council of Ten was a terrible strutting fellow with a rapier-like nose, a buff leather jerkin and a trailing scarlet cloak that the crowd was careful not to step on.

It was all vastly diverting, and Tony would gladly have gone on forever; but he had given his word to the captain to be at the landing-place at sunset, and here was dusk already creeping over the skies! Tony was a man of honour; and having pressed on the Count a handsome damascened dagger selected from one of the goldsmiths' shops in a narrow street lined with such wares, he insisted on turning his face toward the Hepzibah's gig. The Count yielded reluctantly; but as they came out again on the square they were caught in a great throng pouring toward the doors of the cathedral.

"They go to Benediction," said the Count. "A beautiful sight, with many lights and flowers. It is a pity you cannot take a peep at it."

Tony thought so too, and in another minute a legless beggar had pulled back the leathern flap of the cathedral door, and they stood in a haze of gold and perfume that seemed to rise and fall on the mighty undulations of the organ. Here the press was as thick as without; and as Tony flattened himself against a pillar, he heard a pretty voice at his elbow:—"Oh, sir, oh, sir, your sword!"

He turned at sound of the broken English, and saw a girl who matched the voice trying to disengage her dress from the tip of his scabbard. She wore one of the voluminous black hoods which the Venetian ladies affected, and under its projecting eaves her face spied out at him as sweet as a nesting bird.

In the dusk their hands met over the scabbard, and as she freed herself a shred of her lace flounce clung to Tony's enchanted fingers. Looking after her, he saw she was on the arm of a pompous-looking graybeard in a long black gown and scarlet stockings, who, on perceiving the exchange of glances between the young people, drew the lady away with a threatening look.

The Count met Tony's eye with a smile. "One of our Venetian beauties," said he; "the lovely Polixena Cador. She is thought to have the finest eyes in Venice."

"She spoke English," stammered Tony.

"Oh—ah—precisely: she learned the language at the Court of Saint James's, where her father, the Senator, was formerly accredited as Ambassador. She played as an infant with the royal princes of England."

"And that was her father?"

"Assuredly: young ladies of Donna Polixena's rank do not go abroad save with their parents or a duenna."

Just then a soft hand slid into Tony's. His heart gave a foolish bound, and he turned about half-expecting to meet again the merry eyes under the hood; but saw instead a slender brown boy, in some kind of fanciful page's dress, who thrust a folded paper between his fingers and vanished in the throng. Tony, in a tingle, glanced surreptitiously at the Count, who appeared absorbed in his prayers. The crowd, at the ringing of a bell, had in fact been overswept by a sudden wave of devotion; and Tony seized the moment to step beneath a lighted shrine with his letter.

"I am in dreadful trouble and implore your help. Polixena"—he read; but hardly had he seized the sense of the words when a hand fell on his shoulder, and a stern-looking man in a cocked hat, and bearing a kind of rod or mace, pronounced a few words in Venetian.

Tony, with a start, thrust the letter in his breast, and tried to jerk himself free; but the harder he jerked the tighter grew the other's grip, and the Count, presently perceiving what had happened, pushed his way through the crowd, and whispered hastily to his companion: "For God's sake, make no struggle. This is serious. Keep quiet and do as I tell you."

Tony was no chicken-heart. He had something of a name for pugnacity among the lads of his own age at home, and was not the man to stand in Venice what he would have resented in Salem; but the devil of it was that this black fellow seemed to be pointing to the letter in his breast; and this suspicion was confirmed by the Count's agitated whisper.

"This is one of the agents of the Ten.—For God's sake, no outcry." He exchanged a word or two with the mace-bearer and again turned to Tony. "You have been seen concealing a letter about your person—"

"And what of that?" says Tony furiously.

"Gently, gently, my master. A letter handed to you by the page of Donna Polixena Cador.—A black business! Oh, a very black business! This Cador is one of the most powerful nobles in Venice—I beseech you, not a word, sir! Let me think—deliberate—"

His hand on Tony's shoulder, he carried on a rapid dialogue with the potentate in the cocked hat.

"I am sorry, sir—but our young ladies of rank are as

jealously guarded as the Grand Turk's wives, and you must be answerable for this scandal. The best I can do is to have you taken privately to the Palazzo Cador, instead of being brought before the Council. I have pleaded your youth and inexperience"—Tony winced at this—"and I think the business may still be arranged."

Meanwhile the agent of the Ten had yielded his place to a sharp-featured shabby-looking fellow in black, dressed somewhat like a lawyer's clerk, who laid a grimy hand on Tony's arm, and with many apologetic gestures steered him through the crowd to the doors of the church. The Count held him by the other arm, and in this fashion they emerged on the square, which now lay in darkness save for the many lights twinkling under the arcade and in the windows of the gaming-rooms above it.

Tony by this time had regained voice enough to declare that he would go where they pleased, but that he must first say a word to the mate of the Hepzibah, who had now been awaiting him some two hours or more at the landing-place.

The Count repeated this to Tony's custodian, but the latter shook his head and rattled off a sharp denial.

"Impossible, sir," said the Count. "I entreat you not to insist. Any resistance will tell against you in the end."

Tony fell silent. With a rapid eye he was measuring his chances of escape. In wind and limb he was more than a mate for his captors, and boyhood's ruses were not so far behind him but he felt himself equal to outwitting a dozen grown men; but he had the sense to see that at a cry the crowd would close in on him. Space was what he wanted: a clear ten yards, and he would have laughed at Doge and Council. But the throng was thick as glue, and he walked on submissively, keeping his eye alert for an opening. Suddenly the mob swerved aside after some new show. Tony's fist shot out at the black fellow's chest, and before the latter could right himself the young New Englander was showing a clean pair of heels to his escort. On he sped, cleaving the crowd like a flood-tide in Gloucester bay, diving under the first arch that caught his eye, dashing down a lane to an unlit water-way, and plunging across a narrow hump-back bridge which landed him in a black pocket between walls. But now his pursuers were at his back, reinforced by the yelping mob. The walls were too high to scale, and for all his courage Tony's breath came short as he paced the masonry cage in which ill-luck had landed him. Suddenly a gate opened in one of the walls, and a slip of a servant wench looked out and beckoned him. There was no time to weigh chances. Tony dashed through the gate, his rescuer slammed and bolted it, and the two stood in a narrow paved well between high houses.

CHAPTER II

The servant picked up a lantern and signed to Tony to follow her. They climbed a squalid stairway of stone, felt their way along a corridor, and entered a tall vaulted room feebly lit by an oil-lamp hung from the painted ceiling. Tony discerned traces of former splendour in his surroundings, but he had no time to examine them, for a figure started up at his approach and in the dim light he recognized the girl who was the cause of all his troubles.

She sprang toward him with outstretched hands, but as he advanced her face changed and she shrank back abashed.

"This is a misunderstanding—a dreadful misunderstanding," she cried out in her pretty broken English. "Oh, how does it happen that you are here?"

"Through no choice of my own, madam, I assure you!" retorted Tony, not over-pleased by his reception.

"But why—how—how did you make this unfortunate mistake?"

"Why, madam, if you'll excuse my candour, I think the mistake was yours—"

"Mine?"

—"in sending me a letter—"

"YOU—a letter?"

—"by a simpleton of a lad, who must needs hand it to me under your father's very nose—"

The girl broke in on him with a cry. "What! It was YOU who received my letter?" She swept round on the little maid-servant and submerged her under a flood of Venetian. The latter volleyed back in the same jargon, and as she did so, Tony's astonished eye detected in her the doubleted page who had handed him the letter in Saint Mark's.

"What!" he cried, "the lad was this girl in disguise?"

Polixena broke off with an irrepressible smile; but her face clouded instantly and she returned to the charge.

"This wicked, careless girl—she has ruined me, she will be my undoing! Oh, sir, how can I make you understand? The letter was not intended for you—it was meant for the English Ambassador, an old friend of my mother's, from whom I hoped to obtain assistance—oh, how can I ever excuse myself to you?"

"No excuses are needed, madam," said Tony, bowing; "though I am surprised, I own, that any one should mistake me for an ambassador."

Here a wave of mirth again overran Polixena's face. "Oh, sir, you must pardon my poor girl's mistake. She heard you speaking English, and—and—I had told her to hand the letter to the handsomest foreigner in the church." Tony bowed again, more profoundly. "The English Ambassador," Polixena added simply, "is a very handsome man."

"I wish, madam, I were a better proxy!"

She echoed his laugh, and then clapped her hands together

with a look of anguish. "Fool that I am! How can I jest at such a moment? I am in dreadful trouble, and now perhaps I have brought trouble on you also— Oh, my father! I hear my father coming!" She turned pale and leaned tremblingly upon the little servant.

Footsteps and loud voices were in fact heard outside, and a moment later the red-stockinged Senator stalked into the room attended by half-a-dozen of the magnificoes whom Tony had seen abroad in the square. At sight of him, all clapped hands to their swords and burst into furious outcries; and though their jargon was unintelligible to the young man, their tones and gestures made their meaning unpleasantly plain. The Senator, with a start of anger, first flung himself on the intruder; then, snatched back by his companions, turned wrathfully on his daughter, who, at his feet, with outstretched arms and streaming face, pleaded her cause with all the eloquence of young distress. Meanwhile the other nobles gesticulated vehemently among themselves, and one, a truculent-looking personage in ruff and Spanish cape, stalked apart, keeping a jealous eye on Tony. The latter was at his wit's end how to comport himself, for the lovely Polixena's tears had quite drowned her few words of English, and beyond guessing that the magnificoes meant him a mischief he had no notion what they would be at.

At this point, luckily, his friend Count Rialto suddenly broke in on the scene, and was at once assailed by all the tongues in the room. He pulled a long face at sight of Tony, but signed to the young man to be silent, and addressed himself earnestly to the Senator. The latter, at first, would not draw breath to hear him; but presently, sobering, he walked apart with the Count, and the two conversed together out of earshot.

"My dear sir," said the Count, at length turning to Tony with a perturbed countenance, "it is as I feared, and you are fallen into a great misfortune."

"A great misfortune! A great trap, I call it!" shouted Tony, whose blood, by this time, was boiling; but as he uttered the word the beautiful Polixena cast such a stricken look on him that he blushed up to the forehead.

"Be careful," said the Count, in a low tone. "Though his Illustriousness does not speak your language, he understands a few words of it, and——"

"So much the better!" broke in Tony; "I hope he will understand me if I ask him in plain English what is his grievance against me."

The Senator, at this, would have burst forth again; but the Count, stepping between, answered quickly: "His grievance against you is that you have been detected in secret correspondence with his daughter, the most noble Polixena Cador, the betrothed bride of this gentleman, the most illustrious Marquess Zanipolo——" and he waved a deferential hand at the frowning hidalgo of the cape and ruff.

"Sir," said Tony, "if that is the extent of my offence, it lies with the young lady to set me free, since by her own avowal—" but here he stopped short, for, to his surprise, Polixena shot a terrified glance at him.

"Sir," interposed the Count, "we are not accustomed in Venice to take shelter behind a lady's reputation."

"No more are we in Salem," retorted Tony in a white heat. "I was merely about to remark that, by the young lady's avowal, she has never seen me before."

Polixena's eyes signalled her gratitude, and he felt he would have died to defend her.

The Count translated his statement, and presently pursued: "His Illustriousness observes that, in that case, his daughter's misconduct has been all the more reprehensible."

"Her misconduct? Of what does he accuse her?"

"Of sending you, just now, in the church of Saint Mark's, a letter which you were seen to read openly and thrust in your bosom. The incident was witnessed by his Illustriousness the Marquess Zanipolo, who, in consequence, has already repudiated his unhappy bride."

Tony stared contemptuously at the black Marquess. "If his Illustriousness is so lacking in gallantry as to repudiate a lady on so trivial a pretext, it is he and not I who should be the object of her father's resentment."

"That, my dear young gentleman, is hardly for you to decide. Your only excuse being your ignorance of our customs, it is scarcely for you to advise us how to behave in matters of punctilio."

It seemed to Tony as though the Count were going over to his enemies, and the thought sharpened his retort.

"I had supposed," said he, "that men of sense had much the same behaviour in all countries, and that, here as elsewhere, a gentleman would be taken at his word. I solemnly affirm that the letter I was seen to read reflects in no way on the honour of this young lady, and has in fact nothing to do with what you suppose."

As he had himself no notion what the letter was about, this was as far as he dared commit himself.

There was another brief consultation in the opposing camp, and the Count then said:—"We all know, sir, that a gentleman is obliged to meet certain enquiries by a denial; but you have at your command the means of immediately clearing the lady. Will you show the letter to her father?"

There was a perceptible pause, during which Tony, while appearing to look straight before him, managed to deflect an interrogatory glance toward Polixena. Her reply was a faint negative motion, accompanied by unmistakable signs of apprehension.

"Poor girl!" he thought, "she is in a worse case than I imagined, and whatever happens I must keep her secret."

He turned to the Senator with a deep bow. "I am not," said he, "in the habit of showing my private correspondence to strangers."

The Count interpreted these words, and Donna Polixena's father, dashing his hand on his hilt, broke into furious invective, while the Marquess continued to nurse his outraged feelings aloof.

The Count shook his head funereally. "Alas, sir, it is as I feared. This is not the first time that youth and propinquity have led to fatal imprudence. But I need hardly, I suppose, point out the obligation incumbent upon you as a man of honour."

Tony stared at him haughtily, with a look which was meant for the Marquess. "And what obligation is that?"

"To repair the wrong you have done—in other words, to marry the lady."

Polixena at this burst into tears, and Tony said to himself: "Why in heaven does she not bid me show the letter?" Then he remembered that it had no superscription, and that the words it contained, supposing them to have been addressed to himself, were hardly of a nature to disarm suspicion. The sense of the girl's grave plight effaced all thought of his own risk, but the Count's last words struck him as so preposterous that he could not repress a smile.

"I cannot flatter myself," said he, "that the lady would welcome this solution."

The Count's manner became increasingly ceremonious. "Such modesty," he said, "becomes your youth and inexperience; but even if it were justified it would scarcely alter the case, as it is always assumed in this country that a young lady wishes to marry the man whom her father has selected."

"But I understood just now," Tony interposed, "that the gentleman yonder was in that enviable position."

"So he was, till circumstances obliged him to waive the privilege in your favour."

"He does me too much honour; but if a deep sense of my unworthiness obliges me to decline—"

"You are still," interrupted the Count, "labouring under a misapprehension. Your choice in the matter is no more to be consulted than the lady's. Not to put too fine a point on it, it is necessary that you should marry her within the hour."

Tony, at this, for all his spirit, felt the blood run thin in his veins. He looked in silence at the threatening visages between himself and the door, stole a side-glance at the high barred windows of the apartment, and then turned to Polixena, who had fallen sobbing at her father's feet.

"And if I refuse?" said he.

The Count made a significant gesture. "I am not so foolish as to threaten a man of your mettle. But perhaps you are unaware what the consequences would be to the lady."

Polixena, at this, struggling to her feet, addressed a few impassioned words to the Count and her father; but the latter put her aside with an obdurate gesture.

The Count turned to Tony. "The lady herself pleads for you—at what cost you do not guess—but as you see it is vain. In an hour his Illustriousness's chaplain will be here. Meanwhile his Illustriousness consents to leave you in the custody of your betrothed."

He stepped back, and the other gentlemen, bowing with deep ceremony to Tony, stalked out one by one from the room. Tony heard the key turn in the lock, and found himself alone with Polixena.

CHAPTER III

The girl had sunk into a chair, her face hidden, a picture of shame and agony. So moving was the sight that Tony once again forgot his own extremity in the view of her distress. He went and kneeled beside her, drawing her hands from her face.

"Oh, don't make me look at you!" she sobbed; but it was on his bosom that she hid from his gaze. He held her there a breathing-space, as he might have clasped a weeping child; then she drew back and put him gently from her.

"What humiliation!" she lamented.

"Do you think I blame you for what has happened?"

"Alas, was it not my foolish letter that brought you to this plight? And how nobly you defended me! How generous it was of you not to show the letter! If my father knew I had written to the Ambassador to save me from this dreadful marriage his anger against me would be even greater."

"Ah—it was that you wrote for?" cried Tony with unaccountable relief.

"Of course—what else did you think?"

"But is it too late for the Ambassador to save you?"

"From YOU?" A smile flashed through her tears. "Alas, yes." She drew back and hid her face again, as though overcome by a fresh wave of shame.

Tony glanced about him. "If I could wrench a bar out of

that window—" he muttered.

"Impossible! The court is guarded. You are a prisoner, alas.—Oh, I must speak!" She sprang up and paced the room. "But indeed you can scarce think worse of me than you do already—"

"I think ill of you?"

"Alas, you must! To be unwilling to marry the man my father has chosen for me—"

"Such a beetle-browed lout! It would be a burning shame if you married him."

"Ah, you come from a free country. Here a girl is allowed no choice."

"It is infamous, I say—infamous!"

"No, no—I ought to have resigned myself, like so many others."

"Resigned yourself to that brute! Impossible!"

"He has a dreadful name for violence—his gondolier has told my little maid such tales of him! But why do I talk of myself, when it is of you I should be thinking?"

"Of me, poor child?" cried Tony, losing his head.

"Yes, and how to save you—for I CAN save you! But every moment counts—and yet what I have to say is so dreadful."

"Nothing from your lips could seem dreadful."

"Ah, if he had had your way of speaking!"

"Well, now at least you are free of him," said Tony, a little wildly; but at this she stood up and bent a grave look on him.

"No, I am not free," she said; "but you are, if you will do as I tell you."

Tony, at this, felt a sudden dizziness; as though, from a mad flight through clouds and darkness, he had dropped to safety again, and the fall had stunned him.

"What am I to do?" he said.

"Look away from me, or I can never tell you."

He thought at first that this was a jest, but her eyes commanded him, and reluctantly he walked away and leaned in the embrasure of the window. She stood in the middle of the room, and as soon as his back was turned she began to speak in a quick monotonous voice, as though she were reciting a lesson.

"You must know that the Marquess Zanipolo, though a great noble, is not a rich man. True, he has large estates, but he is a desperate spendthrift and gambler, and would sell his soul for a round sum of ready money.—If you turn round I shall not go on!—He wrangled horribly with my father over my dowry—he wanted me to have more than either of my sisters, though one married a Procurator and the other a grandee of Spain. But my father is a gambler too—oh, such fortunes as are squandered over the arcade yonder! And so—and so—don't turn, I implore you—oh, do you begin to see my meaning?"

She broke off sobbing, and it took all his strength to keep

his eyes from her.

"Go on," he said.

"Will you not understand? Oh, I would say anything to save you! You don't know us Venetians—we're all to be bought for a price. It is not only the brides who are marketable— sometimes the husbands sell themselves too. And they think you rich—my father does, and the others—I don't know why, unless you have shown your money too freely—and the English are all rich, are they not? And—oh, oh—do you understand? Oh, I can't bear your eyes!"

She dropped into a chair, her head on her arms, and Tony in a flash was at her side.

"My poor child, my poor Polixena!" he cried, and wept and clasped her.

"You ARE rich, are you not? You would promise them a ransom?" she persisted.

"To enable you to marry the Marquess?"

"To enable you to escape from this place. Oh, I hope I may never see your face again." She fell to weeping once more, and he drew away and paced the floor in a fever.

Presently she sprang up with a fresh air of resolution, and pointed to a clock against the wall. "The hour is nearly over. It is quite true that my father is gone to fetch his chaplain. Oh, I implore you, be warned by me! There is no other way of escape."

"And if I do as you say—?"

"You are safe! You are free! I stake my life on it."

"And you—you are married to that villain?"

"But I shall have saved you. Tell me your name, that I may say it to myself when I am alone."

"My name is Anthony. But you must not marry that fellow."

"You forgive me, Anthony? You don't think too badly of me?"

"I say you must not marry that fellow."

She laid a trembling hand on his arm. "Time presses," she adjured him, "and I warn you there is no other way."

For a moment he had a vision of his mother, sitting very upright, on a Sunday evening, reading Dr. Tillotson's sermons in the best parlour at Salem; then he swung round on the girl and caught both her hands in his. "Yes, there is," he cried, "if you are willing. Polixena, let the priest come!"

She shrank back from him, white and radiant. "Oh, hush, be silent!" she said.

"I am no noble Marquess, and have no great estates," he cried. "My father is a plain India merchant in the colony of Massachusetts—but if you—"

"Oh, hush, I say! I don't know what your long words mean. But I bless you, bless you, bless you on my knees!" And she knelt before him, and fell to kissing his hands.

He drew her up to his breast and held her there.

"You are willing, Polixena?" he said.

"No, no!" She broke from him with outstretched hands. "I am not willing. You mistake me. I must marry the Marquess, I tell you!"

"On my money?" he taunted her; and her burning blush rebuked him.

"Yes, on your money," she said sadly.

"Why? Because, much as you hate him, you hate me still more?"

She was silent.

"If you hate me, why do you sacrifice yourself for me?" he persisted.

"You torture me! And I tell you the hour is past."

"Let it pass. I'll not accept your sacrifice. I will not lift a finger to help another man to marry you."

"Oh, madman, madman!" she murmured.

Tony, with crossed arms, faced her squarely, and she leaned against the wall a few feet off from him. Her breast throbbed under its lace and falbalas, and her eyes swam with terror and entreaty.

"Polixena, I love you!" he cried.

A blush swept over her throat and bosom, bathing her in light to the verge of her troubled brows.

"I love you! I love you!" he repeated.

And now she was on his breast again, and all their youth was in their lips. But her embrace was as fleeting as a bird's poise and before he knew it he clasped empty air, and half the room was between them.

She was holding up a little coral charm and laughing. "I took it from your fob," she said. "It is of no value, is it? And I shall not get any of the money, you know."

She continued to laugh strangely, and the rouge burned like fire in her ashen face.

"What are you talking of?" he said.

"They never give me anything but the clothes I wear. And I shall never see you again, Anthony!" She gave him a dreadful look. "Oh, my poor boy, my poor love—'I LOVE YOU, I LOVE YOU, POLIXENA!'"

He thought she had turned light-headed, and advanced to her with soothing words; but she held him quietly at arm's length, and as he gazed he read the truth in her face.

He fell back from her, and a sob broke from him as he bowed his head on his hands.

"Only, for God's sake, have the money ready, or there may be foul play here," she said.

As she spoke there was a great tramping of steps outside and a burst of voices on the threshold.

"It is all a lie," she gasped out, "about my marriage, and the Marquess, and the Ambassador, and the Senator—but not, oh, not about your danger in this place—or about my love," she breathed to him. And as the key rattled in the door she laid her lips on his brow.

The key rattled, and the door swung open—but the black-cassocked gentleman who stepped in, though a priest indeed, was no votary of idolatrous rites, but that sound orthodox divine, the Reverend Ozias Mounce, looking very much perturbed at his surroundings, and very much on the alert for the Scarlet Woman. He was supported, to his evident relief, by the captain of the Hepzibah B., and the procession was closed by an escort of stern-looking fellows in cocked hats and small-swords, who led between them Tony's late friends the magnificoes, now as sorry a looking company as the law ever landed in her net.

The captain strode briskly into the room, uttering a grunt of satisfaction as he clapped eyes on Tony.

"So, Mr. Bracknell," said he, "you have been seeing the Carnival with this pack of mummers, have you? And this is where your pleasuring has landed you? H'm—a pretty establishment, and a pretty lady at the head of it." He glanced about the apartment and doffed his hat with mock ceremony to Polixena, who faced him like a princess.

"Why, my girl," said he, amicably, "I think I saw you this morning in the square, on the arm of the Pantaloon yonder; and as for that Captain Spavent—" and he pointed a derisive finger at the Marquess—"I've watched him drive his bully's trade under the arcade ever since I first dropped anchor in these waters. Well, well," he continued, his indignation subsiding, "all's fair in Carnival, I suppose, but this gentleman here is under sailing orders, and I fear we must break up your little party."

At this Tony saw Count Rialto step forward, looking very small and explanatory, and uncovering obsequiously to the captain.

"I can assure you, sir," said the Count in his best English, "that this incident is the result of an unfortunate misunderstanding, and if you will oblige us by dismissing these myrmidons, any of my friends here will be happy to offer satisfaction to Mr. Bracknell and his companions."

Mr. Mounce shrank visibly at this, and the captain burst into a loud guffaw.

"Satisfaction?" says he. "Why, my cock, that's very handsome of you, considering the rope's at your throats. But we'll not take advantage of your generosity, for I fear Mr. Bracknell has already trespassed on it too long. You pack of galley-slaves, you!" he spluttered suddenly, "decoying young innocents with that devil's bait of yours—" His eye fell on Polixena, and his voice softened unaccountably. "Ah, well, we must all see the Carnival once, I suppose," he said. "All's well that ends well, as the fellow says in the play; and now, if you please, Mr. Bracknell, if you'll take the reverend gentleman's arm there, we'll bid adieu to our hospitable entertainers, and right about face for the Hepzibah."

THE END OF A VENETIAN NIGHT'S ENTERTAINMENT

XINGU

December, 1911

CHAPTER I

Mrs. Ballinger is one of the ladies who pursue Culture in bands, as though it were dangerous to meet alone. To this end she had founded the Lunch Club, an association composed of herself and several other indomitable huntresses of erudition. The Lunch Club, after three or four winters of lunching and debate, had acquired such local distinction that the entertainment of distinguished strangers became one of its accepted functions; in recognition of which it duly extended to the celebrated "Osric Dane," on the day of her arrival in Hillbridge, an invitation to be present at the next meeting.

The Club was to meet at Mrs. Ballinger's. The other members, behind her back, were of one voice in deploring her unwillingness to cede her rights in favor of Mrs. Plinth, whose house made a more impressive setting for the entertainment of celebrities; while, as Mrs. Leveret observed, there was always the picture-gallery to fall back on.

Mrs. Plinth made no secret of sharing this view. She had always regarded it as one of her obligations to entertain the Lunch Club's distinguished guests. Mrs. Plinth was almost as proud of her obligations as she was of her picture-gallery; she was in fact fond of implying that the one possession implied the other, and that only a woman of her wealth could afford to live up to a standard as high as that which she had set herself. An all-round sense of duty, roughly adaptable to various ends, was, in her opinion, all that Providence exacted of the more humbly stationed; but the power which had predestined Mrs. Plinth to keep footmen clearly intended her to maintain an equally specialized staff of responsibilities. It was the more to be regretted that Mrs. Ballinger, whose obligations to society were bounded by the narrow scope of two parlour-maids, should have been so tenacious of the right to entertain Osric Dane.

The question of that lady's reception had for a month past profoundly moved the members of the Lunch Club. It was not that they felt themselves unequal to the task, but that their sense of the opportunity plunged them into the agreeable uncertainty of the lady who weighs the alternatives of a well-stocked wardrobe. If such subsidiary members as Mrs. Leveret were fluttered by the thought of exchanging ideas with the author of "The Wings of Death," no forebodings of the kind disturbed the conscious adequacy of Mrs. Plinth, Mrs. Ballinger and Miss Van Vluyck. "The Wings of Death" had, in fact, at Miss Van Vluyck's suggestion, been chosen as the subject of discussion at the last club meeting, and each member had thus been enabled to express her own opinion or to appropriate whatever seemed most likely to be of use in the comments of the others. Mrs. Roby alone had abstained from profiting by the opportunity thus offered; but it was now openly recognised that, as a member of the Lunch Club, Mrs. Roby was a failure. "It all comes," as Miss Van Vluyck put it, "of accepting a woman on a man's estimation." Mrs. Roby, returning to Hillbridge from a prolonged sojourn in exotic regions—the other ladies no longer took the trouble to remember where—had been emphatically commended by the distinguished biologist, Professor Foreland, as the most agreeable woman he had ever met; and the members of the Lunch Club, awed by an encomium that carried the weight of a diploma, and rashly assuming that the Professor's social sympathies would follow the line of his scientific bent, had seized the chance of annexing a biological member. Their disillusionment was complete. At Miss Van Vluyck's first off-hand mention of the pterodactyl Mrs. Roby had confusedly murmured: "I know so little about metres—" and after that painful betrayal of incompetence she had prudently withdrawn from farther participation in the mental gymnastics of the club.

"I suppose she flattered him," Miss Van Vluyck summed up—"or else it's the way she does her hair."

The dimensions of Miss Van Vluyck's dining-room having restricted the membership of the club to six, the non-conductiveness of one member was a serious obstacle to the exchange of ideas, and some wonder had already been expressed that Mrs. Roby should care to live, as it were, on the intellectual bounty of the others. This feeling was augmented by the discovery that she had not yet read "The Wings of Death." She owned to having heard the name of Osric Dane; but that—incredible as it appeared—was the extent of her acquaintance with the celebrated novelist. The ladies could not conceal their surprise, but Mrs. Ballinger, whose pride in the club made her wish to put even Mrs. Roby in the best possible light, gently insinuated that, though she had not had time to acquaint herself with "The Wings of Death," she must at least be familiar with its equally remarkable predecessor, "The Supreme Instant."

Mrs. Roby wrinkled her sunny brows in a conscientious effort of memory, as a result of which she recalled that, oh, yes, she HAD seen the book at her brother's, when she was staying with him in Brazil, and had even carried it off to read one day on a boating party; but they had all got to shying things at each other in the boat, and the book had gone overboard, so she had never had the chance—

The picture evoked by this anecdote did not advance Mrs. Roby's credit with the club, and there was a painful pause, which was broken by Mrs. Plinth's remarking: "I can understand that, with all your other pursuits, you should not find much time for reading; but I should have thought you might at least have GOT UP 'The Wings of Death' before

Osric Dane's arrival."

Mrs. Roby took this rebuke good-humouredly. She had meant, she owned to glance through the book; but she had been so absorbed in a novel of Trollope's that—

"No one reads Trollope now," Mrs. Ballinger interrupted impatiently.

Mrs. Roby looked pained. "I'm only just beginning," she confessed.

"And does he interest you?" Mrs. Plinth inquired.

"He amuses me."

"Amusement," said Mrs. Plinth sententiously, "is hardly what I look for in my choice of books."

"Oh, certainly, 'The Wings of Death' is not amusing," ventured Mrs. Leveret, whose manner of putting forth an opinion was like that of an obliging salesman with a variety of other styles to submit if his first selection does not suit.

"Was it MEANT to be?" enquired Mrs. Plinth, who was fond of asking questions that she permitted no one but herself to answer. "Assuredly not."

"Assuredly not—that is what I was going to say," assented Mrs. Leveret, hastily rolling up her opinion and reaching for another. "It was meant to—to elevate."

Miss Van Vluyck adjusted her spectacles as though they were the black cap of condemnation. "I hardly see," she interposed, "how a book steeped in the bitterest pessimism can be said to elevate, however much it may instruct."

"I meant, of course, to instruct," said Mrs. Leveret, flurried by the unexpected distinction between two terms which she had supposed to be synonymous. Mrs. Leveret's enjoyment of the Lunch Club was frequently marred by such surprises; and not knowing her own value to the other ladies as a mirror for their mental complacency she was sometimes troubled by a doubt of her worthiness to join in their debates. It was only the fact of having a dull sister who thought her clever that saved her from a sense of hopeless inferiority.

"Do they get married in the end?" Mrs. Roby interposed.

"They—who?" the Lunch Club collectively exclaimed.

"Why, the girl and man. It's a novel, isn't it? I always think that's the one thing that matters. If they're parted it spoils my dinner."

Mrs. Plinth and Mrs. Ballinger exchanged scandalised glances, and the latter said: "I should hardly advise you to read 'The Wings of Death,' in that spirit. For my part, when there are so many books that one HAS to read, I wonder how any one can find time for those that are merely amusing."

"The beautiful part of it," Laura Glyde murmured, "is surely just this—that no one can tell HOW 'The Wings of Death' ends. Osric Dane, overcome by the dread significance of her own meaning, has mercifully veiled it—perhaps even from herself—as Apelles, in representing the sacrifice of Iphigenia, veiled the face of Agamemnon."

"What's that? Is it poetry?" whispered Mrs. Leveret

nervously to Mrs. Plinth, who, disdaining a definite reply, said coldly: "You should look it up. I always make it a point to look things up." Her tone added—"though I might easily have it done for me by the footman."

"I was about to say," Miss Van Vluyck resumed, "that it must always be a question whether a book CAN instruct unless it elevates."

"Oh—" murmured Mrs. Leveret, now feeling herself hopelessly astray.

"I don't know," said Mrs. Ballinger, scenting in Miss Van Vluyck's tone a tendency to depreciate the coveted distinction of entertaining Osric Dane; "I don't know that such a question can seriously be raised as to a book which has attracted more attention among thoughtful people than any novel since 'Robert Elsmere.'"

"Oh, but don't you see," exclaimed Laura Glyde, "that it's just the dark hopelessness of it all—the wonderful tone-scheme of black on black—that makes it such an artistic achievement? It reminded me so when I read it of Prince Rupert's maniere noire... the book is etched, not painted, yet one feels the colour values so intensely..."

"Who is HE?" Mrs. Leveret whispered to her neighbour. "Some one she's met abroad?"

"The wonderful part of the book," Mrs. Ballinger conceded, "is that it may be looked at from so many points of view. I hear that as a study of determinism Professor Lupton ranks it with 'The Data of Ethics.'"

"I'm told that Osric Dane spent ten years in preparatory studies before beginning to write it," said Mrs. Plinth. "She looks up everything—verifies everything. It has always been my principle, as you know. Nothing would induce me, now, to put aside a book before I'd finished it, just because I can buy as many more as I want."

"And what do YOU think of 'The Wings of Death'?" Mrs. Roby abruptly asked her.

It was the kind of question that might be termed out of order, and the ladies glanced at each other as though disclaiming any share in such a breach of discipline. They all knew that there was nothing Mrs. Plinth so much disliked as being asked her opinion of a book. Books were written to read; if one read them what more could be expected? To be questioned in detail regarding the contents of a volume seemed to her as great an outrage as being searched for smuggled laces at the Custom House. The club had always respected this idiosyncrasy of Mrs. Plinth's. Such opinions as she had were imposing and substantial: her mind, like her house, was furnished with monumental "pieces" that were not meant to be suddenly disarranged; and it was one of the unwritten rules of the Lunch Club that, within her own province, each member's habits of thought should be respected. The meeting therefore closed with an increased sense, on the part of the other ladies, of Mrs. Roby's hopeless unfitness to be one of them.

CHAPTER II

Mrs. Leveret, on the eventful day, had arrived early at Mrs. Ballinger's, her volume of Appropriate Allusions in her pocket.

It always flustered Mrs. Leveret to be late at the Lunch Club: she liked to collect her thoughts and gather a hint, as the others assembled, of the turn the conversation was likely to take. To-day, however, she felt herself completely at a loss; and even the familiar contact of Appropriate Allusions, which stuck into her as she sat down, failed to give her any reassurance. It was an admirable little volume, compiled to meet all the social emergencies; so that, whether on the occasion of Anniversaries, joyful or melancholy (as the classification ran), of Banquets, social or municipal, or of Baptisms, Church of England or sectarian, its student need never be at a loss for a pertinent reference. Mrs. Leveret, though she had for years devoutly conned its pages, valued it, however, rather for its moral support than for its practical services; for though in the privacy of her own room she commanded an army of quotations, these invariably deserted her at the critical moment, and the only line she retained—CANST THOU DRAW OUT LEVIATHAN WITH A HOOK?—was one she had never yet found the occasion to apply.

To-day she felt that even the complete mastery of the

volume would hardly have insured her self-possession; for she thought it probable, even if she DID, in some miraculous way, remember an Allusion, it would be only to find that Osric Dane used a different volume (Mrs. Leveret was convinced that literary people always carried them), and would consequently not recognise her quotations.

Mrs. Leveret's sense of being adrift was intensified by the appearance of Mrs. Ballinger's drawing-room. To a careless eye its aspect was unchanged; but those acquainted with Mrs. Ballinger's way of arranging her books would instantly have detected the marks of recent perturbation. Mrs. Ballinger's province, as a member of the Lunch Club, was the Book of the Day. On that, whatever it was, from a novel to a treatise on experimental psychology, she was confidently, authoritatively "up." What became of last year's books, or last week's even; what she did with the "subjects" she had previously professed with equal authority; no one had ever yet discovered. Her mind was an hotel where facts came and went like transient lodgers, without leaving their address behind, and frequently without paying for their board. It was Mrs. Ballinger's boast that she was "abreast with the Thought of the Day," and her pride that this advanced position should be expressed by the books on her drawing-room table. These volumes, frequently renewed, and almost always damp from the press, bore names generally unfamiliar to Mrs. Leveret, and giving her, as she furtively scanned them, a disheartening glimpse of new fields of knowledge to be breathlessly traversed in Mrs. Ballinger's wake. But to-day a number of maturer-looking volumes were adroitly mingled with the primeurs of the press—Karl Marx jostled Professor Bergson, and the "Confessions of St. Augustine" lay beside the last work on "Mendelism"; so that even to Mrs. Leveret's fluttered perceptions it was clear that Mrs. Ballinger didn't in the least know what Osric Dane was likely to talk about, and had taken measures to be prepared for anything. Mrs. Leveret felt like a passenger on an ocean steamer who is told that there is no immediate danger, but that she had better put on her life-belt.

It was a relief to be roused from these forebodings by Miss Van Vluyck's arrival.

"Well, my dear," the new-comer briskly asked her hostess, "what subjects are we to discuss to-day?"

Mrs. Ballinger was furtively replacing a volume of Wordsworth by a copy of Verlaine. "I hardly know," she said somewhat nervously. "Perhaps we had better leave that to circumstances."

"Circumstances?" said Miss Van Vluyck drily. "That means, I suppose, that Laura Glyde will take the floor as usual, and we shall be deluged with literature."

Philanthropy and statistics were Miss Van Vluyck's province, and she naturally resented any tendency to divert their guest's attention from these topics.

Mrs. Plinth at this moment appeared.

"Literature?" she protested in a tone of remonstrance. "But this is perfectly unexpected. I understood we were to talk of Osric Dane's novel."

Mrs. Ballinger winced at the discrimination, but let it pass. "We can hardly make that our chief subject—at least not TOO intentionally," she suggested. "Of course we can let our talk DRIFT in that direction; but we ought to have some other topic as an introduction, and that is what I wanted to consult you about. The fact is, we know so little of Osric Dane's tastes and interests that it is difficult to make any special preparation."

"It may be difficult," said Mrs. Plinth with decision, "but it is absolutely necessary. I know what that happy-go-lucky principle leads to. As I told one of my nieces the other day, there are certain emergencies for which a lady should always be prepared. It's in shocking taste to wear colours when one pays a visit of condolence, or a last year's dress when there are reports that one's husband is on the wrong side of the market; and so it is with conversation. All I ask is that I should know beforehand what is to be talked about; then I feel sure of being able to say the proper thing."

"I quite agree with you," Mrs. Ballinger anxiously assented; "but—"

And at that instant, heralded by the fluttered parlour-maid, Osric Dane appeared upon the threshold.

Mrs. Leveret told her sister afterward that she had known at a glance what was coming. She saw that Osric Dane was not going to meet them half way. That distinguished personage had indeed entered with an air of compulsion not calculated to promote the easy exercise of hospitality. She looked as though she were about to be photographed for a new edition of her books.

The desire to propitiate a divinity is generally in inverse ratio to its responsiveness, and the sense of discouragement produced by Osric Dane's entrance visibly increased the Lunch Club's eagerness to please her. Any lingering idea that she might consider herself under an obligation to her entertainers was at once dispelled by her manner: as Mrs. Leveret said afterward to her sister, she had a way of looking at you that made you feel as if there was something wrong with your hat. This evidence of greatness produced such an immediate impression on the ladies that a shudder of awe ran through them when Mrs. Roby, as their hostess led the great personage into the dining-room, turned back to whisper to the others: "What a brute she is!"

The hour about the table did not tend to correct this verdict. It was passed by Osric Dane in the silent deglutition of Mrs. Ballinger's menu, and by the members of the Club in the emission of tentative platitudes which their guest seemed to swallow as perfunctorily as the successive courses of the luncheon.

Mrs. Ballinger's deplorable delay in fixing a topic had thrown the Club into a mental disarray which increased with the return to the drawing-room, where the actual business of discussion was to open. Each lady waited for the other to speak; and there was a general shock of disappointment when their hostess opened the conversation by the painfully commonplace inquiry: "Is this your first visit to Hillbridge?"

Even Mrs. Leveret was conscious that this was a bad beginning; and a vague impulse of deprecation made Miss Glyde interject: "It is a very small place indeed."

Mrs. Plinth bristled. "We have a great many representative people," she said, in the tone of one who speaks for her order.

Osric Dane turned to her thoughtfully. "What do they represent?" she asked.

Mrs. Plinth's constitutional dislike to being questioned was intensified by her sense of unpreparedness; and her reproachful glance passed the question on to Mrs. Ballinger.

"Why," said that lady, glancing in turn at the other members, "as a community I hope it is not too much to say that we stand for culture."

"For art—" Miss Glyde eagerly interjected.

"For art and literature," Mrs. Ballinger emended.

"And for sociology, I trust," snapped Miss Van Vluyck.

"We have a standard," said Mrs. Plinth, feeling herself suddenly secure on the vast expanse of a generalisation: and Mrs. Leveret, thinking there must be room for more than one on so broad a statement, took courage to murmur: "Oh, certainly; we have a standard."

"The object of our little club," Mrs. Ballinger continued, "is to concentrate the highest tendencies of Hillbridge—to centralise and focus its complex intellectual effort."

This was felt to be so happy that the ladies drew an almost audible breath of relief.

"We aspire," the President went on, "to stand for what is highest in art, literature and ethics."

Osric Dane again turned to her. "What ethics?" she asked.

A tremor of apprehension encircled the room. None of the ladies required any preparation to pronounce on a question of morals; but when they were called ethics it was different. The club, when fresh from the "Encyclopaedia Britannica," the "Reader's Handbook" or Smith's "Classical Dictionary," could deal confidently with any subject; but when taken unawares it had been known to define agnosticism as a heresy of the Early Church and Professor Froude as a distinguished histologist; and such minor members as Mrs. Leveret still secretly regarded ethics as something vaguely pagan.

Even to Mrs. Ballinger, Osric Dane's question was unsettling, and there was a general sense of gratitude when Laura Glyde leaned forward to say, with her most sympathetic accent: "You must excuse us, Mrs. Dane, for not being able, just at present, to talk of anything but 'The Wings of Death.'"

"Yes," said Miss Van Vluyck, with a sudden resolve to carry the war into the enemy's camp. "We are so anxious to know the exact purpose you had in mind in writing your wonderful book."

"You will find," Mrs. Plinth interposed, "that we are not superficial readers."

"We are eager to hear from you," Miss Van Vluyck continued, "if the pessimistic tendency of the book is an expression of your own convictions or—"

"Or merely," Miss Glyde hastily thrust in, "a sombre background brushed in to throw your figures into more vivid relief. ARE you not primarily plastic?"

"I have always maintained," Mrs. Ballinger interposed, "that you represent the purely objective method—"

Osric Dane helped herself critically to coffee. "How do you define objective?" she then inquired.

There was a flurried pause before Laura Glyde intensely murmured: "In reading YOU we don't define, we feel."

Osric Dane smiled. "The cerebellum," she remarked, "is not infrequently the seat of the literary emotions." And she took a second lump of sugar.

The sting that this remark was vaguely felt to conceal was

almost neutralised by the satisfaction of being addressed in such technical language.

"Ah, the cerebellum," said Miss Van Vluyck complacently. "The Club took a course in psychology last winter."

"Which psychology?" asked Osric Dane.

There was an agonising pause, during which each member of the Club secretly deplored the distressing inefficiency of the others. Only Mrs. Roby went on placidly sipping her chartreuse. At last Mrs. Ballinger said, with an attempt at a high tone: "Well, really, you know, it was last year that we took psychology, and this winter we have been so absorbed in—"

She broke off, nervously trying to recall some of the Club's discussions; but her faculties seemed to be paralysed by the petrifying stare of Osric Dane. What HAD the club been absorbed in lately? Mrs. Ballinger, with a vague purpose of gaining time, repeated slowly: "We've been so intensely absorbed in—"

Mrs. Roby put down her liqueur glass and drew near the group with a smile.

"In Xingu?" she gently prompted.

A thrill ran through the other members. They exchanged confused glances, and then, with one accord, turned a gaze of mingled relief and interrogation on their unexpected rescuer. The expression of each denoted a different phase of the same emotion. Mrs. Plinth was the first to compose her features to an air of reassurance: after a moment's hasty adjustment her look almost implied that it was she who had given the word to Mrs. Ballinger.

"Xingu, of course!" exclaimed the latter with her accustomed promptness, while Miss Van Vluyck and Laura Glyde seemed to be plumbing the depths of memory, and Mrs. Leveret, feeling apprehensively for Appropriate Allusions, was somehow reassured by the uncomfortable pressure of its bulk against her person.

Osric Dane's change of countenance was no less striking than that of her entertainers. She too put down her coffee-cup, but with a look of distinct annoyance: she too wore, for a brief moment, what Mrs. Roby afterward described as the look of feeling for something in the back of her head; and before she could dissemble these momentary signs of weakness, Mrs. Roby, turning to her with a deferential smile, had said: "And we've been so hoping that to-day you would tell us just what you think of it."

Osric Dane received the homage of the smile as a matter of course; but the accompanying question obviously embarrassed her, and it became clear to her observers that she was not quick at shifting her facial scenery. It was as though her countenance had so long been set in an expression of unchallenged superiority that the muscles had stiffened, and refused to obey her orders.

"Xingu—" she murmured, as if seeking in her turn to gain

time.

Mrs. Roby continued to press her. "Knowing how engrossing the subject is, you will understand how it happens that the Club has let everything else go to the wall for the moment. Since we took up Xingu I might almost say—were it not for your books—that nothing else seems to us worth remembering."

Osric Dane's stern features were darkened rather than lit up by an uneasy smile. "I am glad to hear there is one exception," she gave out between narrowed lips.

"Oh, of course," Mrs. Roby said prettily; "but as you have shown us that—so very naturally!—you don't care to talk about your own things, we really can't let you off from telling us exactly what you think about Xingu; especially," she added, with a persuasive smile, "as some people say that one of your last books was simply saturated with it."

It was an IT, then—the assurance sped like fire through the parched minds of the other members. In their eagerness to gain the least little clue to Xingu they almost forgot the joy of assisting at the discomfiture of Mrs. Dane.

The latter reddened nervously under her antagonist's direct assault. "May I ask," she faltered out in an embarrassed tone, "to which of my books you refer?"

Mrs. Roby did not falter. "That's just what I want you to tell us; because, though I was present, I didn't actually take part."

"Present at what?" Mrs. Dane took her up; and for an instant the trembling members of the Lunch Club thought that the champion Providence had raised up for them had lost a point. But Mrs. Roby explained herself gaily: "At the discussion, of course. And so we're dreadfully anxious to know just how it was that you went into the Xingu."

There was a portentous pause, a silence so big with incalculable dangers that the members with one accord checked the words on their lips, like soldiers dropping their arms to watch a single combat between their leaders. Then Mrs. Dane gave expression to their inmost dread by saying sharply: "Ah—you say THE Xingu, do you?"

Mrs. Roby smiled undauntedly. "It IS a shade pedantic, isn't it? Personally, I always drop the article; but I don't know how the other members feel about it."

The other members looked as though they would willingly have dispensed with this deferential appeal to their opinion, and Mrs. Roby, after a bright glance about the group, went on: "They probably think, as I do, that nothing really matters except the thing itself—except Xingu."

No immediate reply seemed to occur to Mrs. Dane, and Mrs. Ballinger gathered courage to say: "Surely every one must feel that about Xingu."

Mrs. Plinth came to her support with a heavy murmur of assent, and Laura Glyde breathed emotionally: "I have known cases where it has changed a whole life."

"It has done me worlds of good," Mrs. Leveret interjected, seeming to herself to remember that she had either taken it or read it in the winter before.

"Of course," Mrs. Roby admitted, "the difficulty is that one must give up so much time to it. It's very long."

"I can't imagine," said Miss Van Vluyck tartly, "grudging the time given to such a subject."

"And deep in places," Mrs. Roby pursued; (so then it was a book!) "And it isn't easy to skip."

"I never skip," said Mrs. Plinth dogmatically.

"Ah, it's dangerous to, in Xingu. Even at the start there are places where one can't. One must just wade through."

"I should hardly call it WADING," said Mrs. Ballinger sarcastically.

Mrs. Roby sent her a look of interest. "Ah—you always found it went swimmingly?"

Mrs. Ballinger hesitated. "Of course there are difficult passages," she conceded modestly.

"Yes; some are not at all clear—even," Mrs. Roby added, "if one is familiar with the original."

"As I suppose you are?" Osric Dane interposed, suddenly fixing her with a look of challenge.

Mrs. Roby met it by a deprecating smile. "Oh, it's really not difficult up to a certain point; though some of the branches are very little known, and it's almost impossible to get at the source."

"Have you ever tried?" Mrs. Plinth enquired, still distrustful of Mrs. Roby's thoroughness.

Mrs. Roby was silent for a moment; then she replied with lowered lids: "No—but a friend of mine did; a very brilliant man; and he told me it was best for women—not to..."

A shudder ran around the room. Mrs. Leveret coughed so that the parlour-maid, who was handing the cigarettes, should not hear; Miss Van Vluyck's face took on a nauseated expression, and Mrs. Plinth looked as if she were passing some one she did not care to bow to. But the most remarkable result of Mrs. Roby's words was the effect they produced on the Lunch Club's distinguished guest. Osric Dane's impassive features suddenly melted to an expression of the warmest human sympathy, and edging her chair toward Mrs. Roby's she asked: "Did he really? And—did you find he was right?"

Mrs. Ballinger, in whom annoyance at Mrs. Roby's unwonted assumption of prominence was beginning to displace gratitude for the aid she had rendered, could not consent to her being allowed, by such dubious means, to monopolise the attention of their guest. If Osric Dane had not enough self-respect to resent Mrs. Roby's flippancy, at least the Lunch Club would do so in the person of its President.

Mrs. Ballinger laid her hand on Mrs. Roby's arm. "We must not forget," she said with a frigid amiability, "that absorbing as Xingu is to US, it may be less interesting to—"

"Oh, no, on the contrary, I assure you," Osric Dane energetically intervened.

"—to others," Mrs. Ballinger finished firmly; "and we must not allow our little meeting to end without persuading Mrs. Dane to say a few words to us on a subject which, to-day, is much more present in all our thoughts. I refer, of course, to 'The Wings of Death.'"

The other members, animated by various degrees of the same sentiment, and encouraged by the humanised mien of their redoubtable guest, repeated after Mrs. Ballinger: "Oh, yes, you really MUST talk to us a little about your book."

Osric Dane's expression became as bored, though not as haughty, as when her work had been previously mentioned. But before she could respond to Mrs. Ballinger's request, Mrs. Roby had risen from her seat, and was pulling her veil down over her frivolous nose.

"I'm so sorry," she said, advancing toward her hostess with outstretched hand, "but before Mrs. Dane begins I think I'd better run away. Unluckily, as you know, I haven't read her books, so I should be at a terrible disadvantage among you all; and besides, I've an engagement to play bridge."

If Mrs. Roby had simply pleaded her ignorance of Osric Dane's works as a reason for withdrawing, the Lunch Club, in view of her recent prowess, might have approved such evidence of discretion; but to couple this excuse with the brazen announcement that she was foregoing the privilege for the purpose of joining a bridge-party, was only one more instance of her deplorable lack of discrimination.

The ladies were disposed, however, to feel that her departure—now that she had performed the sole service she was ever likely to render them—would probably make for greater order and dignity in the impending discussion, besides relieving them of the sense of self-distrust which her presence always mysteriously produced. Mrs. Ballinger therefore restricted herself to a formal murmur of regret, and the other members were just grouping themselves comfortably about Osric Dane when the latter, to their dismay, started up from the sofa on which she had been deferentially enthroned.

"Oh wait—do wait, and I'll go with you!" she called out to Mrs. Roby; and, seizing the hands of the disconcerted members, she administered a series of farewell pressures with the mechanical haste of a railway-conductor punching tickets.

"I'm so sorry—I'd quite forgotten—" she flung back at them from the threshold; and as she joined Mrs. Roby, who had turned in surprise at her appeal, the other ladies had the mortification of hearing her say, in a voice which she did not take the pains to lower: "If you'll let me walk a little way with you, I should so like to ask you a few more questions about Xingu..."

CHAPTER III

The incident had been so rapid that the door closed on the departing pair before the other members had had time to understand what was happening. Then a sense of the indignity put upon them by Osric Dane's unceremonious desertion began to contend with the confused feeling that they had been cheated out of their due without exactly knowing how or why.

There was an awkward silence, during which Mrs. Ballinger, with a perfunctory hand, rearranged the skilfully grouped literature at which her distinguished guest had not so much as glanced; then Miss Van Vluyck tartly pronounced: "Well, I can't say that I consider Osric Dane's departure a great loss."

This confession crystallised the fluid resentment of the other members, and Mrs. Leveret exclaimed: "I do believe she came on purpose to be nasty!"

It was Mrs. Plinth's private opinion that Osric Dane's attitude toward the Lunch Club might have been very different had it welcomed her in the majestic setting of the Plinth drawing-rooms; but not liking to reflect on the inadequacy of Mrs. Ballinger's establishment she sought a round-about satisfaction in depreciating her savoir faire.

"I said from the first that we ought to have had a subject ready. It's what always happens when you're unprepared.

Now if we'd only got up Xingu—"

The slowness of Mrs. Plinth's mental processes was always allowed for by the Club; but this instance of it was too much for Mrs. Ballinger's equanimity.

"Xingu!" she scoffed. "Why, it was the fact of our knowing so much more about it than she did—unprepared though we were—that made Osric Dane so furious. I should have thought that was plain enough to everybody!"

This retort impressed even Mrs. Plinth, and Laura Glyde, moved by an impulse of generosity, said: "Yes, we really ought to be grateful to Mrs. Roby for introducing the topic. It may have made Osric Dane furious, but at least it made her civil."

"I am glad we were able to show her," added Miss Van Vluyck, "that a broad and up-to-date culture is not confined to the great intellectual centres."

This increased the satisfaction of the other members, and they began to forget their wrath against Osric Dane in the pleasure of having contributed to her defeat.

Miss Van Vluyck thoughtfully rubbed her spectacles. "What surprised me most," she continued, "was that Fanny Roby should be so up on Xingu."

This frank admission threw a slight chill on the company, but Mrs. Ballinger said with an air of indulgent irony: "Mrs. Roby always has the knack of making a little go a long way; still, we certainly owe her a debt for happening to remember that she'd heard of Xingu." And this was felt by the other members to be a graceful way of cancelling once for all the Club's obligation to Mrs. Roby.

Even Mrs. Leveret took courage to speed a timid shaft of irony: "I fancy Osric Dane hardly expected to take a lesson in Xingu at Hillbridge!"

Mrs. Ballinger smiled. "When she asked me what we represented—do you remember?—I wish I'd simply said we represented Xingu!"

All the ladies laughed appreciatively at this sally, except Mrs. Plinth, who said, after a moment's deliberation: "I'm not sure it would have been wise to do so."

Mrs. Ballinger, who was already beginning to feel as if she had launched at Osric Dane the retort which had just occurred to her, looked ironically at Mrs. Plinth. "May I ask why?" she enquired.

Mrs. Plinth looked grave. "Surely," she said, "I understood from Mrs. Roby herself that the subject was one it was as well not to go into too deeply?"

Miss Van Vluyck rejoined with precision: "I think that applied only to an investigation of the origin of the—of the—"; and suddenly she found that her usually accurate memory had failed her. "It's a part of the subject I never studied myself," she concluded lamely.

"Nor I," said Mrs. Ballinger.

Laura Glyde bent toward them with widened eyes. "And

yet it seems—doesn't it?—the part that is fullest of an esoteric fascination?"

"I don't know on what you base that," said Miss Van Vluyck argumentatively.

"Well, didn't you notice how intensely interested Osric Dane became as soon as she heard what the brilliant foreigner—he WAS a foreigner, wasn't he?—had told Mrs. Roby about the origin—the origin of the rite—or whatever you call it?"

Mrs. Plinth looked disapproving, and Mrs. Ballinger visibly wavered. Then she said in a decisive tone: "It may not be desirable to touch on the—on that part of the subject in general conversation; but, from the importance it evidently has to a woman of Osric Dane's distinction, I feel as if we ought not to be afraid to discuss it among ourselves—without gloves—though with closed doors, if necessary."

"I'm quite of your opinion," Miss Van Vluyck came briskly to her support; "on condition, that is, that all grossness of language is avoided."

"Oh, I'm sure we shall understand without that," Mrs. Leveret tittered; and Laura Glyde added significantly: "I fancy we can read between the lines," while Mrs. Ballinger rose to assure herself that the doors were really closed.

Mrs. Plinth had not yet given her adhesion. "I hardly see," she began, "what benefit is to be derived from investigating such peculiar customs—"

But Mrs. Ballinger's patience had reached the extreme limit of tension. "This at least," she returned; "that we shall not be placed again in the humiliating position of finding ourselves less up on our own subjects than Fanny Roby!"

Even to Mrs. Plinth this argument was conclusive. She peered furtively about the room and lowered her commanding tones to ask: "Have you got a copy?"

"A—a copy?" stammered Mrs. Ballinger. She was aware that the other members were looking at her expectantly, and that this answer was inadequate, so she supported it by asking another question. "A copy of what?"

Her companions bent their expectant gaze on Mrs. Plinth, who, in turn, appeared less sure of herself than usual. "Why, of—of—the book," she explained.

"What book?" snapped Miss Van Vluyck, almost as sharply as Osric Dane.

Mrs. Ballinger looked at Laura Glyde, whose eyes were interrogatively fixed on Mrs. Leveret. The fact of being deferred to was so new to the latter that it filled her with an insane temerity. "Why, Xingu, of course!" she exclaimed.

A profound silence followed this direct challenge to the resources of Mrs. Ballinger's library, and the latter, after glancing nervously toward the Books of the Day, returned in a deprecating voice: "It's not a thing one cares to leave about."

"I should think NOT!" exclaimed Mrs. Plinth.

"It IS a book, then?" said Miss Van Vluyck.

This again threw the company into disarray, and Mrs. Ballinger, with an impatient sigh, rejoined: "Why—there IS a book—naturally..."

"Then why did Miss Glyde call it a religion?"

Laura Glyde started up. "A religion? I never—"

"Yes, you did," Miss Van Vluyck insisted; "you spoke of rites; and Mrs. Plinth said it was a custom."

Miss Glyde was evidently making a desperate effort to reinforce her statement; but accuracy of detail was not her strongest point. At length she began in a deep murmur: "Surely they used to do something of the kind at the Eleusinian mysteries—"

"Oh—" said Miss Van Vluyck, on the verge of disapproval; and Mrs. Plinth protested: "I understood there was to be no indelicacy!"

Mrs. Ballinger could not control her irritation. "Really, it is too bad that we should not be able to talk the matter over quietly among ourselves. Personally, I think that if one goes into Xingu at all—"

"Oh, so do I!" cried Miss Glyde.

"And I don't see how one can avoid doing so, if one wishes to keep up with the Thought of the Day—"

Mrs. Leveret uttered an exclamation of relief. "There—that's it!" she interposed.

"What's it?" the President curtly took her up.

"Why—it's a—a Thought: I mean a philosophy."

This seemed to bring a certain relief to Mrs. Ballinger and Laura Glyde, but Miss Van Vluyck said dogmatically: "Excuse me if I tell you that you're all mistaken. Xingu happens to be a language."

"A language!" the Lunch Club cried.

"Certainly. Don't you remember Fanny Roby's saying that there were several branches, and that some were hard to trace? What could that apply to but dialects?"

Mrs. Ballinger could no longer restrain a contemptuous laugh. "Really, if the Lunch Club has reached such a pass that it has to go to Fanny Roby for instruction on a subject like Xingu, it had almost better cease to exist!"

"It's really her fault for not being clearer," Laura Glyde put in.

"Oh, clearness and Fanny Roby!" Mrs. Ballinger shrugged. "I daresay we shall find she was mistaken on almost every point."

"Why not look it up?" said Mrs. Plinth.

As a rule this recurrent suggestion of Mrs. Plinth's was ignored in the heat of discussion, and only resorted to afterward in the privacy of each member's home. But on the present occasion the desire to ascribe their own confusion of thought to the vague and contradictory nature of Mrs. Roby's statements caused the members of the Lunch Club to utter a collective demand for a book of reference.

At this point the production of her treasured volume gave Mrs. Leveret, for a moment, the unusual experience of occupying the centre front; but she was not able to hold it long, for Appropriate Allusions contained no mention of Xingu.

"Oh, that's not the kind of thing we want!" exclaimed Miss Van Vluyck. She cast a disparaging glance over Mrs. Ballinger's assortment of literature, and added impatiently: "Haven't you any useful books?"

"Of course I have," replied Mrs. Ballinger indignantly; "but I keep them in my husband's dressing-room."

From this region, after some difficulty and delay, the parlour-maid produced the W-Z volume of an Encyclopaedia and, in deference to the fact that the demand for it had come from Miss Van Vluyck, laid the ponderous tome before her.

There was a moment of painful suspense while Miss Van Vluyck rubbed her spectacles, adjusted them, and turned to Z; and a murmur of surprise when she said: "It isn't here."

"I suppose," said Mrs. Plinth, "it's not fit to be put in a book of reference."

"Oh, nonsense!" exclaimed Mrs. Ballinger. "Try X."

Miss Van Vluyck turned back through the volume, peering short-sightedly up and down the pages, till she came to a stop and remained motionless, like a dog on a point.

"Well, have you found it?" Mrs. Ballinger enquired, after a considerable delay.

"Yes. I've found it," said Miss Van Vluyck in a queer voice.

Mrs. Plinth hastily interposed: "I beg you won't read it aloud if there's anything offensive."

Miss Van Vluyck, without answering, continued her silent scrutiny.

"Well, what IS it?" exclaimed Laura Glyde excitedly.

"DO tell us!" urged Mrs. Leveret, feeling that she would have something awful to tell her sister.

Miss Van Vluyck pushed the volume aside and turned slowly toward the expectant group.

"It's a river."

"A RIVER?"

"Yes: in Brazil. Isn't that where she's been living?"

"Who? Fanny Roby? Oh, but you must be mistaken. You've been reading the wrong thing," Mrs. Ballinger exclaimed, leaning over her to seize the volume.

"It's the only XINGU in the Encyclopaedia; and she HAS been living in Brazil," Miss Van Vluyck persisted.

"Yes: her brother has a consulship there," Mrs. Leveret eagerly interposed.

"But it's too ridiculous! I—we—why we ALL remember studying Xingu last year—or the year before last," Mrs. Ballinger stammered.

"I thought I did when YOU said so," Laura Glyde avowed.

"I said so?" cried Mrs. Ballinger.

"Yes. You said it had crowded everything else out of your mind."

"Well, YOU said it had changed your whole life!"

"For that matter, Miss Van Vluyck said she had never grudged the time she'd given it."

Mrs. Plinth interposed: "I made it clear that I knew nothing whatever of the original."

Mrs. Ballinger broke off the dispute with a groan. "Oh, what does it all matter if she's been making fools of us? I believe Miss Van Vluyck's right—she was talking of the river all the while!"

"How could she? It's too preposterous," Miss Glyde exclaimed.

"Listen." Miss Van Vluyck had repossessed herself of the Encyclopaedia, and restored her spectacles to a nose reddened by excitement. "'The Xingu, one of the principal rivers of Brazil, rises on the plateau of Mato Grosso, and flows in a northerly direction for a length of no less than one thousand one hundred and eighteen miles, entering the Amazon near the mouth of the latter river. The upper course of the Xingu is auriferous and fed by numerous branches. Its source was first discovered in 1884 by the German explorer von den Steinen, after a difficult and dangerous expedition through a region inhabited by tribes still in the Stone Age of culture.'"

The ladies received this communication in a state of stupefied silence from which Mrs. Leveret was the first to rally. "She certainly DID speak of its having branches."

The word seemed to snap the last thread of their incredulity. "And of its great length," gasped Mrs. Ballinger.

"She said it was awfully deep, and you couldn't skip—you just had to wade through," Miss Glyde subjoined.

The idea worked its way more slowly through Mrs. Plinth's compact resistances. "How could there be anything improper about a river?" she inquired.

"Improper?"

"Why, what she said about the source—that it was corrupt?"

"Not corrupt, but hard to get at," Laura Glyde corrected. "Some one who'd been there had told her so. I daresay it was the explorer himself—doesn't it say the expedition was dangerous?"

"'Difficult and dangerous,'" read Miss Van Vluyck.

Mrs. Ballinger pressed her hands to her throbbing temples. "There's nothing she said that wouldn't apply to a river—to this river!" She swung about excitedly to the other members. "Why, do you remember her telling us that she hadn't read 'The Supreme Instant' because she'd taken it on a boating party while she was staying with her brother, and some one had 'shied' it overboard—'shied' of course was her own expression?"

The ladies breathlessly signified that the expression had not escaped them.

"Well—and then didn't she tell Osric Dane that one of her books was simply saturated with Xingu? Of course it was, if some of Mrs. Roby's rowdy friends had thrown it into the river!"

This surprising reconstruction of the scene in which they had just participated left the members of the Lunch Club inarticulate. At length Mrs. Plinth, after visibly labouring with the problem, said in a heavy tone: "Osric Dane was taken in too."

Mrs. Leveret took courage at this. "Perhaps that's what Mrs. Roby did it for. She said Osric Dane was a brute, and she may have wanted to give her a lesson."

Miss Van Vluyck frowned. "It was hardly worth while to do it at our expense."

"At least," said Miss Glyde with a touch of bitterness, "she succeeded in interesting her, which was more than we did."

"What chance had we?" rejoined Mrs. Ballinger. "Mrs. Roby monopolised her from the first. And THAT, I've no doubt, was her purpose—to give Osric Dane a false impression of her own standing in the Club. She would hesitate at nothing to attract attention: we all know how she took in poor Professor Foreland."

"She actually makes him give bridge-teas every Thursday," Mrs. Leveret piped up.

Laura Glyde struck her hands together. "Why, this is Thursday, and it's THERE she's gone, of course; and taken Osric with her!"

"And they're shrieking over us at this moment," said Mrs. Ballinger between her teeth.

This possibility seemed too preposterous to be admitted. "She would hardly dare," said Miss Van Vluyck, "confess the imposture to Osric Dane."

"I'm not so sure: I thought I saw her make a sign as she left. If she hadn't made a sign, why should Osric Dane have rushed out after her?"

"Well, you know, we'd all been telling her how wonderful Xingu was, and she said she wanted to find out more about it," Mrs. Leveret said, with a tardy impulse of justice to the absent.

This reminder, far from mitigating the wrath of the other members, gave it a stronger impetus.

"Yes—and that's exactly what they're both laughing over now," said Laura Glyde ironically.

Mrs. Plinth stood up and gathered her expensive furs about her monumental form. "I have no wish to criticise," she said; "but unless the Lunch Club can protect its members against the recurrence of such—such unbecoming scenes, I for one—"

"Oh, so do I!" agreed Miss Glyde, rising also.

Miss Van Vluyck closed the Encyclopaedia and proceeded

to button herself into her jacket. "My time is really too valuable—" she began.

"I fancy we are all of one mind," said Mrs. Ballinger, looking searchingly at Mrs. Leveret, who looked at the others.

"I always deprecate anything like a scandal—" Mrs. Plinth continued.

"She has been the cause of one to-day!" exclaimed Miss Glyde.

Mrs. Leveret moaned: "I don't see how she COULD!" and Miss Van Vluyck said, picking up her note-book: "Some women stop at nothing."

"—but if," Mrs. Plinth took up her argument impressively, "anything of the kind had happened in MY house" (it never would have, her tone implied), "I should have felt that I owed it to myself either to ask for Mrs. Roby's resignation— or to offer mine."

"Oh, Mrs. Plinth—" gasped the Lunch Club.

"Fortunately for me," Mrs. Plinth continued with an awful magnanimity, "the matter was taken out of my hands by our President's decision that the right to entertain distinguished guests was a privilege vested in her office; and I think the other members will agree that, as she was alone in this opinion, she ought to be alone in deciding on the best way of effacing its—its really deplorable consequences."

A deep silence followed this unexpected outbreak of Mrs. Plinth's long-stored resentment.

"I don't see why I should be expected to ask her to resign—" Mrs. Ballinger at length began; but Laura Glyde turned back to remind her: "You know she made you say that you'd got on swimmingly in Xingu."

An ill-timed giggle escaped from Mrs. Leveret, and Mrs. Ballinger energetically continued "—but you needn't think for a moment that I'm afraid to!"

The door of the drawing-room closed on the retreating backs of the Lunch Club, and the President of that distinguished association, seating herself at her writing-table, and pushing away a copy of "The Wings of Death" to make room for her elbow, drew forth a sheet of the club's note-paper, on which she began to write: "My dear Mrs. Roby—"

THE END OF XINGU

THE VERDICT

June 1908

I had always thought Jack Gisburn rather a cheap genius—though a good fellow enough—so it was no great surprise to me to hear that, in the height of his glory, he had dropped his painting, married a rich widow, and established himself in a villa on the Riviera. (Though I rather thought it would have been Rome or Florence.)

"The height of his glory"—that was what the women called it. I can hear Mrs. Gideon Thwing—his last Chicago sitter—deploring his unaccountable abdication. "Of course it's going to send the value of my picture 'way up; but I don't think of that, Mr. Rickham—the loss to Arrt is all I think of." The word, on Mrs. Thwing's lips, multiplied its RS as though they were reflected in an endless vista of mirrors. And it was not only the Mrs. Thwings who mourned. Had not the exquisite Hermia Croft, at the last Grafton Gallery show, stopped me before Gisburn's "Moon-dancers" to say, with tears in her eyes: "We shall not look upon its like again"?

Well!—even through the prism of Hermia's tears I felt able to face the fact with equanimity. Poor Jack Gisburn! The women had made him—it was fitting that they should mourn him. Among his own sex fewer regrets were heard, and in his own trade hardly a murmur. Professional jealousy?

Perhaps. If it were, the honour of the craft was vindicated by little Claude Nutley, who, in all good faith, brought out in the Burlington a very handsome "obituary" on Jack—one of those showy articles stocked with random technicalities that I have heard (I won't say by whom) compared to Gisburn's painting. And so—his resolve being apparently irrevocable—the discussion gradually died out, and, as Mrs. Thwing had predicted, the price of "Gisburns" went up.

It was not till three years later that, in the course of a few weeks' idling on the Riviera, it suddenly occurred to me to wonder why Gisburn had given up his painting. On reflection, it really was a tempting problem. To accuse his wife would have been too easy—his fair sitters had been denied the solace of saying that Mrs. Gisburn had "dragged him down." For Mrs. Gisburn—as such—had not existed till nearly a year after Jack's resolve had been taken. It might be that he had married her—since he liked his ease—because he didn't want to go on painting; but it would have been hard to prove that he had given up his painting because he had married her.

Of course, if she had not dragged him down, she had equally, as Miss Croft contended, failed to "lift him up"—she had not led him back to the easel. To put the brush into his hand again—what a vocation for a wife! But Mrs. Gisburn appeared to have disdained it—and I felt it might be interesting to find out why.

The desultory life of the Riviera lends itself to such purely academic speculations; and having, on my way to Monte Carlo, caught a glimpse of Jack's balustraded terraces between the pines, I had myself borne thither the next day.

I found the couple at tea beneath their palm-trees; and Mrs. Gisburn's welcome was so genial that, in the ensuing weeks, I claimed it frequently. It was not that my hostess was "interesting": on that point I could have given Miss Croft the fullest reassurance. It was just because she was NOT interesting—if I may be pardoned the bull—that I found her so. For Jack, all his life, had been surrounded by interesting women: they had fostered his art, it had been reared in the hot-house of their adulation. And it was therefore instructive to note what effect the "deadening atmosphere of mediocrity" (I quote Miss Croft) was having on him.

I have mentioned that Mrs. Gisburn was rich; and it was immediately perceptible that her husband was extracting from this circumstance a delicate but substantial satisfaction. It is, as a rule, the people who scorn money who get most out of it; and Jack's elegant disdain of his wife's big balance enabled him, with an appearance of perfect good-breeding, to transmute it into objects of art and luxury. To the latter, I must add, he remained relatively indifferent; but he was buying Renaissance bronzes and eighteenth-century pictures with a discrimination that bespoke the amplest resources.

"Money's only excuse is to put beauty into circulation,"

was one of the axioms he laid down across the Sevres and silver of an exquisitely appointed luncheon-table, when, on a later day, I had again run over from Monte Carlo; and Mrs. Gisburn, beaming on him, added for my enlightenment: "Jack is so morbidly sensitive to every form of beauty."

Poor Jack! It had always been his fate to have women say such things of him: the fact should be set down in extenuation. What struck me now was that, for the first time, he resented the tone. I had seen him, so often, basking under similar tributes—was it the conjugal note that robbed them of their savour? No—for, oddly enough, it became apparent that he was fond of Mrs. Gisburn—fond enough not to see her absurdity. It was his own absurdity he seemed to be wincing under—his own attitude as an object for garlands and incense.

"My dear, since I've chucked painting people don't say that stuff about me—they say it about Victor Grindle," was his only protest, as he rose from the table and strolled out onto the sunlit terrace.

I glanced after him, struck by his last word. Victor Grindle was, in fact, becoming the man of the moment—as Jack himself, one might put it, had been the man of the hour. The younger artist was said to have formed himself at my friend's feet, and I wondered if a tinge of jealousy underlay the latter's mysterious abdication. But no—for it was not till after that event that the rose Dubarry drawing-rooms had begun to display their "Grindles."

I turned to Mrs. Gisburn, who had lingered to give a lump of sugar to her spaniel in the dining-room.

"Why HAS he chucked painting?" I asked abruptly.

She raised her eyebrows with a hint of good-humoured surprise.

"Oh, he doesn't HAVE to now, you know; and I want him to enjoy himself," she said quite simply.

I looked about the spacious white-panelled room, with its famille-verte vases repeating the tones of the pale damask curtains, and its eighteenth-century pastels in delicate faded frames.

"Has he chucked his pictures too? I haven't seen a single one in the house."

A slight shade of constraint crossed Mrs. Gisburn's open countenance. "It's his ridiculous modesty, you know. He says they're not fit to have about; he's sent them all away except one—my portrait—and that I have to keep upstairs."

His ridiculous modesty—Jack's modesty about his pictures? My curiosity was growing like the bean-stalk. I said persuasively to my hostess: "I must really see your portrait, you know."

She glanced out almost timorously at the terrace where her husband, lounging in a hooded chair, had lit a cigar and drawn the Russian deerhound's head between his knees.

"Well, come while he's not looking," she said, with a

laugh that tried to hide her nervousness; and I followed her between the marble Emperors of the hall, and up the wide stairs with terra-cotta nymphs poised among flowers at each landing.

In the dimmest corner of her boudoir, amid a profusion of delicate and distinguished objects, hung one of the familiar oval canvases, in the inevitable garlanded frame. The mere outline of the frame called up all Gisburn's past!

Mrs. Gisburn drew back the window-curtains, moved aside a jardiniere full of pink azaleas, pushed an arm-chair away, and said: "If you stand here you can just manage to see it. I had it over the mantel-piece, but he wouldn't let it stay."

Yes—I could just manage to see it—the first portrait of Jack's I had ever had to strain my eyes over! Usually they had the place of honour—say the central panel in a pale yellow or rose Dubarry drawing-room, or a monumental easel placed so that it took the light through curtains of old Venetian point. The more modest place became the picture better; yet, as my eyes grew accustomed to the half-light, all the characteristic qualities came out—all the hesitations disguised as audacities, the tricks of prestidigitation by which, with such consummate skill, he managed to divert attention from the real business of the picture to some pretty irrelevance of detail. Mrs. Gisburn, presenting a neutral surface to work on—forming, as it were, so inevitably the background of her own picture—had lent herself in an unusual degree to the display of this false virtuosity. The picture was one of Jack's "strongest," as his admirers would have put it—it represented, on his part, a swelling of muscles, a congesting of veins, a balancing, straddling and straining, that reminded one of the circus-clown's ironic efforts to lift a feather. It met, in short, at every point the demand of lovely woman to be painted "strongly" because she was tired of being painted "sweetly"—and yet not to lose an atom of the sweetness.

"It's the last he painted, you know," Mrs. Gisburn said with pardonable pride. "The last but one," she corrected herself—"but the other doesn't count, because he destroyed it."

"Destroyed it?" I was about to follow up this clue when I heard a footstep and saw Jack himself on the threshold.

As he stood there, his hands in the pockets of his velveteen coat, the thin brown waves of hair pushed back from his white forehead, his lean sunburnt cheeks furrowed by a smile that lifted the tips of a self-confident moustache, I felt to what a degree he had the same quality as his pictures—the quality of looking cleverer than he was.

His wife glanced at him deprecatingly, but his eyes travelled past her to the portrait.

"Mr. Rickham wanted to see it," she began, as if excusing herself. He shrugged his shoulders, still smiling.

"Oh, Rickham found me out long ago," he said lightly;

then, passing his arm through mine: "Come and see the rest of the house."

He showed it to me with a kind of naive suburban pride: the bath-rooms, the speaking-tubes, the dress-closets, the trouser-presses—all the complex simplifications of the millionaire's domestic economy. And whenever my wonder paid the expected tribute he said, throwing out his chest a little: "Yes, I really don't see how people manage to live without that."

Well—it was just the end one might have foreseen for him. Only he was, through it all and in spite of it all—as he had been through, and in spite of, his pictures—so handsome, so charming, so disarming, that one longed to cry out: "Be dissatisfied with your leisure!" as once one had longed to say: "Be dissatisfied with your work!"

But, with the cry on my lips, my diagnosis suffered an unexpected check.

"This is my own lair," he said, leading me into a dark plain room at the end of the florid vista. It was square and brown and leathery: no "effects"; no bric-a-brac, none of the air of posing for reproduction in a picture weekly—above all, no least sign of ever having been used as a studio.

The fact brought home to me the absolute finality of Jack's break with his old life.

"Don't you ever dabble with paint any more?" I asked, still looking about for a trace of such activity.

"Never," he said briefly.

"Or water-colour—or etching?"

His confident eyes grew dim, and his cheeks paled a little under their handsome sunburn.

"Never think of it, my dear fellow—any more than if I'd never touched a brush."

And his tone told me in a flash that he never thought of anything else.

I moved away, instinctively embarrassed by my unexpected discovery; and as I turned, my eye fell on a small picture above the mantel-piece—the only object breaking the plain oak panelling of the room.

"Oh, by Jove!" I said.

It was a sketch of a donkey—an old tired donkey, standing in the rain under a wall.

"By Jove—a Stroud!" I cried.

He was silent; but I felt him close behind me, breathing a little quickly.

"What a wonder! Made with a dozen lines—but on everlasting foundations. You lucky chap, where did you get it?"

He answered slowly: "Mrs. Stroud gave it to me."

"Ah—I didn't know you even knew the Strouds. He was such an inflexible hermit."

"I didn't—till after.... She sent for me to paint him when he was dead."

"When he was dead? You?"

I must have let a little too much amazement escape through my surprise, for he answered with a deprecating laugh: "Yes—she's an awful simpleton, you know, Mrs. Stroud. Her only idea was to have him done by a fashionable painter—ah, poor Stroud! She thought it the surest way of proclaiming his greatness—of forcing it on a purblind public. And at the moment I was THE fashionable painter."

"Ah, poor Stroud—as you say. Was THAT his history?"

"That was his history. She believed in him, gloried in him—or thought she did. But she couldn't bear not to have all the drawing-rooms with her. She couldn't bear the fact that, on varnishing days, one could always get near enough to see his pictures. Poor woman! She's just a fragment groping for other fragments. Stroud is the only whole I ever knew."

"You ever knew? But you just said—"

Gisburn had a curious smile in his eyes.

"Oh, I knew him, and he knew me—only it happened after he was dead."

I dropped my voice instinctively. "When she sent for you?"

"Yes—quite insensible to the irony. She wanted him vindicated—and by me!"

He laughed again, and threw back his head to look up at the sketch of the donkey. "There were days when I couldn't look at that thing—couldn't face it. But I forced myself to put it here; and now it's cured me—cured me. That's the reason why I don't dabble any more, my dear Rickham; or rather Stroud himself is the reason."

For the first time my idle curiosity about my companion turned into a serious desire to understand him better.

"I wish you'd tell me how it happened," I said.

He stood looking up at the sketch, and twirling between his fingers a cigarette he had forgotten to light. Suddenly he turned toward me.

"I'd rather like to tell you—because I've always suspected you of loathing my work."

I made a deprecating gesture, which he negatived with a good-humoured shrug.

"Oh, I didn't care a straw when I believed in myself—and now it's an added tie between us!"

He laughed slightly, without bitterness, and pushed one of the deep arm-chairs forward. "There: make yourself comfortable—and here are the cigars you like."

He placed them at my elbow and continued to wander up and down the room, stopping now and then beneath the picture.

"How it happened? I can tell you in five minutes—and it didn't take much longer to happen.... I can remember now how surprised and pleased I was when I got Mrs. Stroud's note. Of course, deep down, I had always FELT there was no one like him—only I had gone with the stream, echoed the usual platitudes about him, till I half got to think he was a failure, one of the kind that are left behind. By Jove, and he WAS left behind—because he had come to stay! The rest of us had to let ourselves be swept along or go under, but he was high above the current—on everlasting foundations, as you say.

"Well, I went off to the house in my most egregious mood—rather moved, Lord forgive me, at the pathos of poor Stroud's career of failure being crowned by the glory of my painting him! Of course I meant to do the picture for nothing—I told Mrs. Stroud so when she began to stammer something about her poverty. I remember getting off a prodigious phrase about the honour being MINE—oh, I was princely, my dear Rickham! I was posing to myself like one of my own sitters.

"Then I was taken up and left alone with him. I had sent all my traps in advance, and I had only to set up the easel and get to work. He had been dead only twenty-four hours, and he died suddenly, of heart disease, so that there had been no preliminary work of destruction—his face was clear and untouched. I had met him once or twice, years before, and thought him insignificant and dingy. Now I saw that he was superb.

"I was glad at first, with a merely aesthetic satisfaction: glad to have my hand on such a 'subject.' Then his strange life-likeness began to affect me queerly—as I blocked the head in I felt as if he were watching me do it. The sensation was followed by the thought: if he WERE watching me, what would he say to my way of working? My strokes began to go a little wild—I felt nervous and uncertain.

"Once, when I looked up, I seemed to see a smile behind his close grayish beard—as if he had the secret, and were amusing himself by holding it back from me. That exasperated me still more. The secret? Why, I had a secret worth twenty of his! I dashed at the canvas furiously, and tried some of my bravura tricks. But they failed me, they crumbled. I saw that he wasn't watching the showy bits—I couldn't distract his attention; he just kept his eyes on the hard passages between. Those were the ones I had always shirked, or covered up with some lying paint. And how he saw through my lies!

"I looked up again, and caught sight of that sketch of the donkey hanging on the wall near his bed. His wife told me afterward it was the last thing he had done—just a note taken with a shaking hand, when he was down in Devonshire recovering from a previous heart attack. Just a note! But it tells his whole history. There are years of patient scornful persistence in every line. A man who had swum with the current could never have learned that mighty upstream stroke....

"I turned back to my work, and went on groping and muddling; then I looked at the donkey again. I saw that, when Stroud laid in the first stroke, he knew just what the end would be. He had possessed his subject, absorbed it, recreated it. When had I done that with any of my things? They hadn't been born of me—I had just adopted them....

"Hang it, Rickham, with that face watching me I couldn't do another stroke. The plain truth was, I didn't know where to put it—I HAD NEVER KNOWN. Only, with my sitters and my public, a showy splash of colour covered up the fact—I just threw paint into their faces.... Well, paint was the one medium those dead eyes could see through—see straight to the tottering foundations underneath. Don't you know how, in talking a foreign language, even fluently, one says half the time not what one wants to but what one can? Well—that was the way I painted; and as he lay there and watched me, the thing they called my 'technique' collapsed like a house of cards. He didn't sneer, you understand, poor Stroud—he just lay there quietly watching, and on his lips, through the gray beard, I seemed to hear the question: 'Are you sure you know where you're coming out?'

"If I could have painted that face, with that question on it, I should have done a great thing. The next greatest thing was to see that I couldn't—and that grace was given me. But, oh, at that minute, Rickham, was there anything on earth I wouldn't have given to have Stroud alive before me, and to hear him say: 'It's not too late—I'll show you how'?

"It WAS too late—it would have been, even if he'd been alive. I packed up my traps, and went down and told Mrs.

Stroud. Of course I didn't tell her THAT—it would have been Greek to her. I simply said I couldn't paint him, that I was too moved. She rather liked the idea—she's so romantic! It was that that made her give me the donkey. But she was terribly upset at not getting the portrait—she did so want him 'done' by some one showy! At first I was afraid she wouldn't let me off—and at my wits' end I suggested Grindle. Yes, it was I who started Grindle: I told Mrs. Stroud he was the 'coming' man, and she told somebody else, and so it got to be true.... And he painted Stroud without wincing; and she hung the picture among her husband's things...."

He flung himself down in the arm-chair near mine, laid back his head, and clasping his arms beneath it, looked up at the picture above the chimney-piece.

"I like to fancy that Stroud himself would have given it to me, if he'd been able to say what he thought that day."

And, in answer to a question I put half-mechanically—"Begin again?" he flashed out. "When the one thing that brings me anywhere near him is that I knew enough to leave off?"

He stood up and laid his hand on my shoulder with a laugh. "Only the irony of it is that I AM still painting—since Grindle's doing it for me! The Strouds stand alone, and happen once—but there's no exterminating our kind of art."

THE END OF THE VERDICT

THE RECKONING

August, 1902

CHAPTER I

"The marriage law of the new dispensation will be: THOU SHALT NOT BE UNFAITHFUL—TO THYSELF."

A discreet murmur of approval filled the studio, and through the haze of cigarette smoke Mrs. Clement Westall, as her husband descended from his improvised platform, saw him merged in a congratulatory group of ladies. Westall's informal talks on "The New Ethics" had drawn about him an eager following of the mentally unemployed—those who, as he had once phrased it, liked to have their brain-food cut up for them. The talks had begun by accident. Westall's ideas were known to be "advanced," but hitherto their advance had not been in the direction of publicity. He had been, in his wife's opinion, almost pusillanimously careful not to let his personal views endanger his professional standing. Of late, however, he had shown a puzzling tendency to dogmatize, to throw down the gauntlet, to flaunt his private code in the face of society; and the relation of the sexes being a topic always sure of an audience, a few admiring friends had persuaded him to give his after-dinner opinions a larger circulation by summing them up in a series of talks at the

161

Van Sideren studio.

The Herbert Van Siderens were a couple who subsisted, socially, on the fact that they had a studio. Van Sideren's pictures were chiefly valuable as accessories to the mise en scene which differentiated his wife's "afternoons" from the blighting functions held in long New York drawing-rooms, and permitted her to offer their friends whiskey-and-soda instead of tea. Mrs. Van Sideren, for her part, was skilled in making the most of the kind of atmosphere which a lay-figure and an easel create; and if at times she found the illusion hard to maintain, and lost courage to the extent of almost wishing that Herbert could paint, she promptly overcame such moments of weakness by calling in some fresh talent, some extraneous re-enforcement of the "artistic" impression. It was in quest of such aid that she had seized on Westall, coaxing him, somewhat to his wife's surprise, into a flattered participation in her fraud. It was vaguely felt, in the Van Sideren circle, that all the audacities were artistic, and that a teacher who pronounced marriage immoral was somehow as distinguished as a painter who depicted purple grass and a green sky. The Van Sideren set were tired of the conventional color-scheme in art and conduct.

Julia Westall had long had her own views on the immorality of marriage; she might indeed have claimed her husband as a disciple. In the early days of their union she had secretly resented his disinclination to proclaim himself a follower of the new creed; had been inclined to tax him with moral cowardice, with a failure to live up to the convictions for which their marriage was supposed to stand. That was in the first burst of propagandism, when, womanlike, she wanted to turn her disobedience into a law. Now she felt differently. She could hardly account for the change, yet being a woman who never allowed her impulses to remain unaccounted for, she tried to do so by saying that she did not care to have the articles of her faith misinterpreted by the vulgar. In this connection, she was beginning to think that almost every one was vulgar; certainly there were few to whom she would have cared to intrust the defence of so esoteric a doctrine. And it was precisely at this point that Westall, discarding his unspoken principles, had chosen to descend from the heights of privacy, and stand hawking his convictions at the street-corner!

It was Una Van Sideren who, on this occasion, unconsciously focussed upon herself Mrs. Westall's wandering resentment. In the first place, the girl had no business to be there. It was "horrid"—Mrs. Westall found herself slipping back into the old feminine vocabulary—simply "horrid" to think of a young girl's being allowed to listen to such talk. The fact that Una smoked cigarettes and sipped an occasional cocktail did not in the least tarnish a certain radiant innocency which made her appear the victim, rather than the accomplice, of her parents' vulgarities. Julia Westall felt in a hot helpless way that something ought to be done—that some one ought to speak to the girl's mother. And just then Una glided up.

"Oh, Mrs. Westall, how beautiful it was!" Una fixed her with large limpid eyes. "You believe it all, I suppose?" she asked with seraphic gravity.

"All—what, my dear child?"

The girl shone on her. "About the higher life—the freer expansion of the individual—the law of fidelity to one's self," she glibly recited.

Mrs. Westall, to her own wonder, blushed a deep and burning blush.

"My dear Una," she said, "you don't in the least understand what it's all about!"

Miss Van Sideren stared, with a slowly answering blush. "Don't YOU, then?" she murmured.

Mrs. Westall laughed. "Not always—or altogether! But I should like some tea, please."

Una led her to the corner where innocent beverages were dispensed. As Julia received her cup she scrutinized the girl more carefully. It was not such a girlish face, after all— definite lines were forming under the rosy haze of youth. She reflected that Una must be six-and-twenty, and wondered why she had not married. A nice stock of ideas she would have as her dower! If THEY were to be a part of the modern girl's trousseau—

Mrs. Westall caught herself up with a start. It was as

though some one else had been speaking—a stranger who had borrowed her own voice: she felt herself the dupe of some fantastic mental ventriloquism. Concluding suddenly that the room was stifling and Una's tea too sweet, she set down her cup, and looked about for Westall: to meet his eyes had long been her refuge from every uncertainty. She met them now, but only, as she felt, in transit; they included her parenthetically in a larger flight. She followed the flight, and it carried her to a corner to which Una had withdrawn—one of the palmy nooks to which Mrs. Van Sideren attributed the success of her Saturdays. Westall, a moment later, had overtaken his look, and found a place at the girl's side. She bent forward, speaking eagerly; he leaned back, listening, with the depreciatory smile which acted as a filter to flattery, enabling him to swallow the strongest doses without apparent grossness of appetite. Julia winced at her own definition of the smile.

On the way home, in the deserted winter dusk, Westall surprised his wife by a sudden boyish pressure of her arm. "Did I open their eyes a bit? Did I tell them what you wanted me to?" he asked gaily.

Almost unconsciously, she let her arm slip from his. "What I wanted—?"

"Why, haven't you—all this time?" She caught the honest wonder of his tone. "I somehow fancied you'd rather blamed me for not talking more openly—before— You've made me feel, at times, that I was sacrificing principles to expediency."

She paused a moment over her reply; then she asked quietly: "What made you decide not to—any longer?"

She felt again the vibration of a faint surprise. "Why—the wish to please you!" he answered, almost too simply.

"I wish you would not go on, then," she said abruptly.

He stopped in his quick walk, and she felt his stare through the darkness.

"Not go on—?"

"Call a hansom, please. I'm tired," broke from her with a sudden rush of physical weariness.

Instantly his solicitude enveloped her. The room had been infernally hot—and then that confounded cigarette smoke— he had noticed once or twice that she looked pale—she mustn't come to another Saturday. She felt herself yielding, as she always did, to the warm influence of his concern for her, the feminine in her leaning on the man in him with a conscious intensity of abandonment. He put her in the hansom, and her hand stole into his in the darkness. A tear or two rose, and she let them fall. It was so delicious to cry over imaginary troubles!

That evening, after dinner, he surprised her by reverting to the subject of his talk. He combined a man's dislike of uncomfortable questions with an almost feminine skill in eluding them; and she knew that if he returned to the subject he must have some special reason for doing so.

"You seem not to have cared for what I said this afternoon. Did I put the case badly?"

"No—you put it very well."

"Then what did you mean by saying that you would rather not have me go on with it?"

She glanced at him nervously, her ignorance of his intention deepening her sense of helplessness.

"I don't think I care to hear such things discussed in public."

"I don't understand you," he exclaimed. Again the feeling that his surprise was genuine gave an air of obliquity to her own attitude. She was not sure that she understood herself.

"Won't you explain?" he said with a tinge of impatience. Her eyes wandered about the familiar drawing-room which had been the scene of so many of their evening confidences. The shaded lamps, the quiet-colored walls hung with mezzotints, the pale spring flowers scattered here and there in Venice glasses and bowls of old Sevres, recalled, she hardly knew why, the apartment in which the evenings of her first marriage had been passed—a wilderness of rosewood and upholstery, with a picture of a Roman peasant above the mantel-piece, and a Greek slave in "statuary marble" between the folding-doors of the back drawing-room. It was a room with which she had never been able to establish any closer relation than that between a traveller and a railway station;

and now, as she looked about at the surroundings which stood for her deepest affinities—the room for which she had left that other room—she was startled by the same sense of strangeness and unfamiliarity. The prints, the flowers, the subdued tones of the old porcelains, seemed to typify a superficial refinement that had no relation to the deeper significances of life.

Suddenly she heard her husband repeating his question.

"I don't know that I can explain," she faltered.

He drew his arm-chair forward so that he faced her across the hearth. The light of a reading-lamp fell on his finely drawn face, which had a kind of surface-sensitiveness akin to the surface-refinement of its setting.

"Is it that you no longer believe in our ideas?" he asked.

"In our ideas—?"

"The ideas I am trying to teach. The ideas you and I are supposed to stand for." He paused a moment. "The ideas on which our marriage was founded."

The blood rushed to her face. He had his reasons, then— she was sure now that he had his reasons! In the ten years of their marriage, how often had either of them stopped to consider the ideas on which it was founded? How often does a man dig about the basement of his house to examine its foundation? The foundation is there, of course—the house rests on it—but one lives abovestairs and not in the cellar. It was she, indeed, who in the beginning had insisted on reviewing the situation now and then, on recapitulating the reasons which justified her course, on proclaiming, from time to time, her adherence to the religion of personal independence; but she had long ceased to feel the need of any such ideal standards, and had accepted her marriage as frankly and naturally as though it had been based on the primitive needs of the heart, and needed no special sanction to explain or justify it.

"Of course I still believe in our ideas!" she exclaimed.

"Then I repeat that I don't understand. It was a part of your theory that the greatest possible publicity should be given to our view of marriage. Have you changed your mind in that respect?"

She hesitated. "It depends on circumstances—on the public one is addressing. The set of people that the Van Siderens get about them don't care for the truth or falseness of a doctrine. They are attracted simply by its novelty."

"And yet it was in just such a set of people that you and I met, and learned the truth from each other."

"That was different."

"In what way?"

"I was not a young girl, to begin with. It is perfectly unfitting that young girls should be present at—at such times—should hear such things discussed—"

"I thought you considered it one of the deepest social wrongs that such things never ARE discussed before young girls; but that is beside the point, for I don't remember seeing any young girl in my audience to-day—"

"Except Una Van Sideren!"

He turned slightly and pushed back the lamp at his elbow.

"Oh, Miss Van Sideren—naturally—"

"Why naturally?"

"The daughter of the house—would you have had her sent out with her governess?"

"If I had a daughter I should not allow such things to go on in my house!"

Westall, stroking his mustache, leaned back with a faint smile. "I fancy Miss Van Sideren is quite capable of taking care of herself."

"No girl knows how to take care of herself—till it's too late."

"And yet you would deliberately deny her the surest means of self-defence?"

"What do you call the surest means of self-defence?"

"Some preliminary knowledge of human nature in its relation to the marriage tie."

She made an impatient gesture. "How should you like to marry that kind of a girl?"

"Immensely—if she were my kind of girl in other respects."

She took up the argument at another point.

"You are quite mistaken if you think such talk does not affect young girls. Una was in a state of the most absurd exaltation—" She broke off, wondering why she had spoken.

Westall reopened a magazine which he had laid aside at the beginning of their discussion. "What you tell me is immensely flattering to my oratorical talent—but I fear you overrate its effect. I can assure you that Miss Van Sideren doesn't have to have her thinking done for her. She's quite capable of doing it herself."

"You seem very familiar with her mental processes!" flashed unguardedly from his wife.

He looked up quietly from the pages he was cutting.

"I should like to be," he answered. "She interests me."

CHAPTER II

If there be a distinction in being misunderstood, it was one denied to Julia Westall when she left her first husband. Every one was ready to excuse and even to defend her. The world she adorned agreed that John Arment was "impossible," and hostesses gave a sigh of relief at the thought that it would no longer be necessary to ask him to dine.

There had been no scandal connected with the divorce: neither side had accused the other of the offence euphemistically described as "statutory." The Arments had indeed been obliged to transfer their allegiance to a State which recognized desertion as a cause for divorce, and construed the term so liberally that the seeds of desertion were shown to exist in every union. Even Mrs. Arment's second marriage did not make traditional morality stir in its sleep. It was known that she had not met her second husband till after she had parted from the first, and she had, moreover, replaced a rich man by a poor one. Though Clement Westall was acknowledged to be a rising lawyer, it was generally felt that his fortunes would not rise as rapidly as his reputation. The Westalls would probably always have to live quietly and go out to dinner in cabs. Could there be better evidence of Mrs. Arment's complete disinterestedness?

If the reasoning by which her friends justified her course was somewhat cruder and less complex than her own elucidation of the matter, both explanations led to the same conclusion: John Arment was impossible. The only difference was that, to his wife, his impossibility was something deeper than a social disqualification. She had once said, in ironical defence of her marriage, that it had at least preserved her from the necessity of sitting next to him at dinner; but she had not then realized at what cost the immunity was purchased. John Arment was impossible; but the sting of his impossibility lay in the fact that he made it impossible for those about him to be other than himself. By an unconscious process of elimination he had excluded from the world everything of which he did not feel a personal need: had become, as it were, a climate in which only his own requirements survived. This might seem to imply a deliberate selfishness; but there was nothing deliberate about Arment. He was as instinctive as an animal or a child. It was this childish element in his nature which sometimes for a moment unsettled his wife's estimate of him. Was it possible that he was simply undeveloped, that he had delayed, somewhat longer than is usual, the laborious process of growing up? He had the kind of sporadic shrewdness which causes it to be said of a dull man that he is "no fool"; and it was this quality that his wife found most trying. Even to the naturalist it is annoying to have his deductions disturbed by some unforeseen aberrancy of form or function; and how much more so to the wife whose estimate of herself is inevitably bound up with her judgment of her husband!

Arment's shrewdness did not, indeed, imply any latent intellectual power; it suggested, rather, potentialities of feeling, of suffering, perhaps, in a blind rudimentary way, on which Julia's sensibilities naturally declined to linger. She so fully understood her own reasons for leaving him that she disliked to think they were not as comprehensible to her husband. She was haunted, in her analytic moments, by the look of perplexity, too inarticulate for words, with which he had acquiesced to her explanations.

These moments were rare with her, however. Her marriage had been too concrete a misery to be surveyed philosophically. If she had been unhappy for complex reasons, the unhappiness was as real as though it had been uncomplicated. Soul is more bruisable than flesh, and Julia was wounded in every fibre of her spirit. Her husband's personality seemed to be closing gradually in on her, obscuring the sky and cutting off the air, till she felt herself shut up among the decaying bodies of her starved hopes. A sense of having been decoyed by some world-old conspiracy into this bondage of body and soul filled her with despair. If marriage was the slow life-long acquittal of a debt contracted in ignorance, then marriage was a crime against human nature. She, for one, would have no share in maintaining the pretence of which she had been a victim: the pretence that a man and a woman, forced into the narrowest of personal relations, must remain there till the end, though they may have outgrown the span of each other's natures as the mature tree outgrows the iron brace about the sapling.

It was in the first heat of her moral indignation that she had met Clement Westall. She had seen at once that he was "interested," and had fought off the discovery, dreading any influence that should draw her back into the bondage of conventional relations. To ward off the peril she had, with an almost crude precipitancy, revealed her opinions to him. To her surprise, she found that he shared them. She was attracted by the frankness of a suitor who, while pressing his suit, admitted that he did not believe in marriage. Her worst audacities did not seem to surprise him: he had thought out all that she had felt, and they had reached the same conclusion. People grew at varying rates, and the yoke that was an easy fit for the one might soon become galling to the other. That was what divorce was for: the readjustment of personal relations. As soon as their necessarily transitive nature was recognized they would gain in dignity as well as in harmony. There would be no farther need of the ignoble concessions and connivances, the perpetual sacrifice of personal delicacy and moral pride, by means of which imperfect marriages were now held together. Each partner to the contract would be on his mettle, forced to live up to the highest standard of self-development, on pain of losing the other's respect and affection. The low nature could no longer drag the higher down, but must struggle to rise, or remain alone on its inferior level. The only necessary condition to a harmonious marriage was a frank recognition of this truth, and a solemn agreement between the contracting parties to keep faith with themselves, and not to live together for a moment after complete accord had ceased to exist between them. The new adultery was unfaithfulness to self.

It was, as Westall had just reminded her, on this understanding that they had married. The ceremony was an unimportant concession to social prejudice: now that the door of divorce stood open, no marriage need be an imprisonment, and the contract therefore no longer involved any diminution of self-respect. The nature of their attachment placed them so far beyond the reach of such contingencies that it was easy to discuss them with an open mind; and Julia's sense of security made her dwell with a tender insistence on Westall's promise to claim his release when he should cease to love her. The exchange of these vows seemed to make them, in a sense, champions of the new law, pioneers in the forbidden realm of individual freedom: they felt that they had somehow achieved beatitude without martyrdom.

This, as Julia now reviewed the past, she perceived to have been her theoretical attitude toward marriage. It was unconsciously, insidiously, that her ten years of happiness with Westall had developed another conception of the tie; a reversion, rather, to the old instinct of passionate dependency and possessorship that now made her blood revolt at the mere hint of change. Change? Renewal? Was that what they had called it, in their foolish jargon? Destruction, extermination rather—this rending of a myriad fibres interwoven with another's being! Another? But he was not other! He and she were one, one in the mystic sense which alone gave marriage its significance. The new law was not for them, but for the disunited creatures forced into a mockery of union. The gospel she had felt called on to proclaim had no bearing on her own case.... She sent for the doctor and told him she was sure she needed a nerve tonic.

She took the nerve tonic diligently, but it failed to act as a sedative to her fears. She did not know what she feared; but that made her anxiety the more pervasive. Her husband had not reverted to the subject of his Saturday talks. He was unusually kind and considerate, with a softening of his quick manner, a touch of shyness in his consideration, that sickened her with new fears. She told herself that it was because she looked badly—because he knew about the doctor and the nerve tonic—that he showed this deference to her wishes, this eagerness to screen her from moral draughts; but the explanation simply cleared the way for fresh inferences.

The week passed slowly, vacantly, like a prolonged Sunday. On Saturday the morning post brought a note from Mrs. Van Sideren. Would dear Julia ask Mr. Westall to come half an hour earlier than usual, as there was to be some music after his "talk"? Westall was just leaving for his office when his wife read the note. She opened the drawing-room door and called him back to deliver the message.

He glanced at the note and tossed it aside. "What a bore! I shall have to cut my game of racquets. Well, I suppose it can't be helped. Will you write and say it's all right?"

Julia hesitated a moment, her hand stiffening on the chair-back against which she leaned.

"You mean to go on with these talks?" she asked.

"I—why not?" he returned; and this time it struck her that his surprise was not quite unfeigned. The discovery helped her to find words.

"You said you had started them with the idea of pleasing me—"

"Well?"

"I told you last week that they didn't please me."

"Last week? Oh—" He seemed to make an effort of memory. "I thought you were nervous then; you sent for the doctor the next day."

"It was not the doctor I needed; it was your assurance—"

"My assurance?"

Suddenly she felt the floor fail under her. She sank into the chair with a choking throat, her words, her reasons slipping away from her like straws down a whirling flood.

"Clement," she cried, "isn't it enough for you to know that I hate it?"

He turned to close the door behind them; then he walked toward her and sat down. "What is it that you hate?" he asked gently.

She had made a desperate effort to rally her routed argument.

"I can't bear to have you speak as if—as if—our marriage—were like the other kind—the wrong kind. When I heard you there, the other afternoon, before all those inquisitive gossiping people, proclaiming that husbands and wives had a right to leave each other whenever they were tired—or had seen some one else— "

Westall sat motionless, his eyes fixed on a pattern of the carpet.

"You HAVE ceased to take this view, then?" he said as she broke off. "You no longer believe that husbands and wives ARE justified in separating—under such conditions?"

"Under such conditions?" she stammered. "Yes—I still believe that—but how can we judge for others? What can we know of the circumstances—?"

He interrupted her. "I thought it was a fundamental article of our creed that the special circumstances produced by marriage were not to interfere with the full assertion of individual liberty." He paused a moment. "I thought that was your reason for leaving Arment."

She flushed to the forehead. It was not like him to give a personal turn to the argument.

"It was my reason," she said simply.

"Well, then—why do you refuse to recognize its validity now?"

"I don't—I don't—I only say that one can't judge for others."

He made an impatient movement. "This is mere hair-splitting. What you mean is that, the doctrine having served your purpose when you needed it, you now repudiate it."

"Well," she exclaimed, flushing again, "what if I do? What does it matter to us?"

Westall rose from his chair. He was excessively pale, and stood before his wife with something of the formality of a stranger.

"It matters to me," he said in a low voice, "because I do NOT repudiate it."

"Well—?"

"And because I had intended to invoke it as"—

He paused and drew his breath deeply. She sat silent, almost deafened by her heart-beats.

—"as a complete justification of the course I am about to take."

Julia remained motionless. "What course is that?" she asked.

He cleared his throat. "I mean to claim the fulfilment of your promise."

For an instant the room wavered and darkened; then she

recovered a torturing acuteness of vision. Every detail of her surroundings pressed upon her: the tick of the clock, the slant of sunlight on the wall, the hardness of the chair-arms that she grasped, were a separate wound to each sense.

"My promise—" she faltered.

"Your part of our mutual agreement to set each other free if one or the other should wish to be released."

She was silent again. He waited a moment, shifting his position nervously; then he said, with a touch of irritability: "You acknowledge the agreement?"

The question went through her like a shock. She lifted her head to it proudly. "I acknowledge the agreement," she said.

"And—you don't mean to repudiate it?"

A log on the hearth fell forward, and mechanically he advanced and pushed it back.

"No," she answered slowly, "I don't mean to repudiate it."

There was a pause. He remained near the hearth, his elbow resting on the mantel-shelf. Close to his hand stood a little cup of jade that he had given her on one of their wedding anniversaries. She wondered vaguely if he noticed it.

"You intend to leave me, then?" she said at length.

His gesture seemed to deprecate the crudeness of the allusion.

"To marry some one else?"

Again his eye and hand protested. She rose and stood

before him.

"Why should you be afraid to tell me? Is it Una Van Sideren?"

He was silent.

"I wish you good luck," she said.

CHAPTER III

She looked up, finding herself alone. She did not remember when or how he had left the room, or how long afterward she had sat there. The fire still smouldered on the hearth, but the slant of sunlight had left the wall.

Her first conscious thought was that she had not broken her word, that she had fulfilled the very letter of their bargain. There had been no crying out, no vain appeal to the past, no attempt at temporizing or evasion. She had marched straight up to the guns.

Now that it was over, she sickened to find herself alive. She looked about her, trying to recover her hold on reality. Her identity seemed to be slipping from her, as it disappears in a physical swoon. "This is my room—this is my house," she heard herself saying. Her room? Her house? She could almost hear the walls laugh back at her.

She stood up, a dull ache in every bone. The silence of the room frightened her. She remembered, now, having heard the front door close a long time ago: the sound suddenly re-echoed through her brain. Her husband must have left the house, then—her HUSBAND? She no longer knew in what terms to think: the simplest phrases had a poisoned edge. She sank back into her chair, overcome by a strange weakness. The clock struck ten—it was only ten o'clock! Suddenly she remembered that she had not ordered dinner...

or were they dining out that evening? DINNER—DINING OUT—the old meaningless phraseology pursued her! She must try to think of herself as she would think of some one else, a some one dissociated from all the familiar routine of the past, whose wants and habits must gradually be learned, as one might spy out the ways of a strange animal...

The clock struck another hour—eleven. She stood up again and walked to the door: she thought she would go up stairs to her room. HER room? Again the word derided her. She opened the door, crossed the narrow hall, and walked up the stairs. As she passed, she noticed Westall's sticks and umbrellas: a pair of his gloves lay on the hall table. The same stair-carpet mounted between the same walls; the same old French print, in its narrow black frame, faced her on the landing. This visual continuity was intolerable. Within, a gaping chasm; without, the same untroubled and familiar surface. She must get away from it before she could attempt to think. But, once in her room, she sat down on the lounge, a stupor creeping over her...

Gradually her vision cleared. A great deal had happened in the interval—a wild marching and countermarching of emotions, arguments, ideas—a fury of insurgent impulses that fell back spent upon themselves. She had tried, at first, to rally, to organize these chaotic forces. There must be help somewhere, if only she could master the inner tumult. Life could not be broken off short like this, for a whim, a fancy;

the law itself would side with her, would defend her. The law? What claim had she upon it? She was the prisoner of her own choice: she had been her own legislator, and she was the predestined victim of the code she had devised. But this was grotesque, intolerable—a mad mistake, for which she could not be held accountable! The law she had despised was still there, might still be invoked... invoked, but to what end? Could she ask it to chain Westall to her side? SHE had been allowed to go free when she claimed her freedom— should she show less magnanimity than she had exacted? Magnanimity? The word lashed her with its irony—one does not strike an attitude when one is fighting for life! She would threaten, grovel, cajole... she would yield anything to keep her hold on happiness. Ah, but the difficulty lay deeper! The law could not help her—her own apostasy could not help her. She was the victim of the theories she renounced. It was as though some giant machine of her own making had caught her up in its wheels and was grinding her to atoms...

It was afternoon when she found herself out-of-doors. She walked with an aimless haste, fearing to meet familiar faces. The day was radiant, metallic: one of those searching American days so calculated to reveal the shortcomings of our street-cleaning and the excesses of our architecture. The streets looked bare and hideous; everything stared and glittered. She called a passing hansom, and gave Mrs. Van Sideren's address. She did not know what had led up to the act; but she found herself suddenly resolved to speak, to cry out a warning. It was too late to save herself—but the girl might still be told. The hansom rattled up Fifth Avenue; she sat with her eyes fixed, avoiding recognition. At the Van Siderens' door she sprang out and rang the bell. Action had cleared her brain, and she felt calm and self-possessed. She knew now exactly what she meant to say.

The ladies were both out... the parlor-maid stood waiting for a card. Julia, with a vague murmur, turned away from the door and lingered a moment on the sidewalk. Then she remembered that she had not paid the cab-driver. She drew a dollar from her purse and handed it to him. He touched his hat and drove off, leaving her alone in the long empty street. She wandered away westward, toward strange thoroughfares, where she was not likely to meet acquaintances. The feeling of aimlessness had returned. Once she found herself in the afternoon torrent of Broadway, swept past tawdry shops and flaming theatrical posters, with a succession of meaningless faces gliding by in the opposite direction...

A feeling of faintness reminded her that she had not eaten since morning. She turned into a side street of shabby houses, with rows of ash-barrels behind bent area railings. In a basement window she saw the sign LADIES' RESTAURANT: a pie and a dish of doughnuts lay against the dusty pane like petrified food in an ethnological museum. She entered, and a young woman with a weak mouth and a brazen eye cleared a table for her near the window. The table was covered with a red and white cotton cloth and adorned with a bunch of celery in a thick tumbler and a salt-cellar full of grayish lumpy salt. Julia ordered tea, and sat a long time waiting for it. She was glad to be away from the noise and confusion of the streets. The low-ceilinged room was empty, and two or three waitresses with thin pert faces lounged in the background staring at her and whispering together. At last the tea was brought in a discolored metal teapot. Julia poured a cup and drank it hastily. It was black and bitter, but it flowed through her veins like an elixir. She was almost dizzy with exhilaration. Oh, how tired, how unutterably tired she had been!

She drank a second cup, blacker and bitterer, and now her mind was once more working clearly. She felt as vigorous, as decisive, as when she had stood on the Van Siderens' door-step—but the wish to return there had subsided. She saw now the futility of such an attempt—the humiliation to which it might have exposed her... The pity of it was that she did not know what to do next. The short winter day was fading, and she realized that she could not remain much longer in the restaurant without attracting notice. She paid for her tea and went out into the street. The lamps were alight, and here and there a basement shop cast an oblong of gas-light across the fissured pavement. In the dusk there was something sinister about the aspect of the street, and she hastened back toward Fifth Avenue. She was not used to being out alone at that hour.

At the corner of Fifth Avenue she paused and stood watching the stream of carriages. At last a policeman caught sight of her and signed to her that he would take her across. She had not meant to cross the street, but she obeyed automatically, and presently found herself on the farther corner. There she paused again for a moment; but she fancied the policeman was watching her, and this sent her hastening down the nearest side street... After that she walked a long time, vaguely... Night had fallen, and now and then, through the windows of a passing carriage, she caught the expanse of an evening waistcoat or the shimmer of an opera cloak...

Suddenly she found herself in a familiar street. She stood still a moment, breathing quickly. She had turned the corner without noticing whither it led; but now, a few yards ahead of her, she saw the house in which she had once lived—her first husband's house. The blinds were drawn, and only a faint translucence marked the windows and the transom above the door. As she stood there she heard a step behind her, and a man walked by in the direction of the house. He walked slowly, with a heavy middle-aged gait, his head sunk a little between the shoulders, the red crease of his neck visible above the fur collar of his overcoat. He crossed the street, went up the steps of the house, drew forth a latch-key, and let himself in...

There was no one else in sight. Julia leaned for a long time against the area-rail at the corner, her eyes fixed on the front of the house. The feeling of physical weariness had returned, but the strong tea still throbbed in her veins and lit her brain with an unnatural clearness. Presently she heard another step draw near, and moving quickly away, she too crossed the street and mounted the steps of the house. The impulse which had carried her there prolonged itself in a quick pressure of the electric bell—then she felt suddenly weak and tremulous, and grasped the balustrade for support. The door opened and a young footman with a fresh inexperienced face stood on the threshold. Julia knew in an instant that he would admit her.

"I saw Mr. Arment going in just now," she said. "Will you ask him to see me for a moment?"

The footman hesitated. "I think Mr. Arment has gone up to dress for dinner, madam."

Julia advanced into the hall. "I am sure he will see me—I will not detain him long," she said. She spoke quietly, authoritatively, in the tone which a good servant does not mistake. The footman had his hand on the drawing-room door.

"I will tell him, madam. What name, please?"

Julia trembled: she had not thought of that. "Merely say a lady," she returned carelessly.

The footman wavered and she fancied herself lost; but at that instant the door opened from within and John Arment stepped into the hall. He drew back sharply as he saw her, his florid face turning sallow with the shock; then the blood poured back to it, swelling the veins on his temples and reddening the lobes of his thick ears.

It was long since Julia had seen him, and she was startled at the change in his appearance. He had thickened, coarsened, settled down into the enclosing flesh. But she noted this insensibly: her one conscious thought was that, now she was face to face with him, she must not let him escape till he had heard her. Every pulse in her body throbbed with the urgency of her message.

She went up to him as he drew back. "I must speak to you," she said.

Arment hesitated, red and stammering. Julia glanced at the footman, and her look acted as a warning. The instinctive shrinking from a "scene" predominated over every other impulse, and Arment said slowly: "Will you come this way?"

He followed her into the drawing-room and closed the door. Julia, as she advanced, was vaguely aware that the room at least was unchanged: time had not mitigated its horrors. The contadina still lurched from the chimney-breast, and the Greek slave obstructed the threshold of the inner room. The place was alive with memories: they started out from every fold of the yellow satin curtains and glided between the angles of the rosewood furniture. But while some subordinate agency was carrying these impressions to her brain, her whole conscious effort was centred in the act of dominating Arment's will. The fear that he would refuse to hear her mounted like fever to her brain. She felt her purpose melt before it, words and arguments running into each other in the heat of her longing. For a moment her voice failed her, and she imagined herself thrust out before she could speak; but as she was struggling for a word, Arment pushed a chair forward, and said quietly: "You are not well."

The sound of his voice steadied her. It was neither kind nor unkind—a voice that suspended judgment, rather, awaiting unforeseen developments. She supported herself against the back of the chair and drew a deep breath. "Shall I send for something?" he continued, with a cold embarrassed politeness.

Julia raised an entreating hand. "No—no—thank you. I am quite well."

He paused midway toward the bell and turned on her. "Then may I ask—?"

"Yes," she interrupted him. "I came here because I wanted to see you. There is something I must tell you."

Arment continued to scrutinize her. "I am surprised at that," he said. "I should have supposed that any communication you may wish to make could have been made through our lawyers."

"Our lawyers!" She burst into a little laugh. "I don't think they could help me—this time."

Arment's face took on a barricaded look. "If there is any question of help—of course—"

It struck her, whimsically, that she had seen that look when some shabby devil called with a subscription-book. Perhaps he thought she wanted him to put his name down for so much in sympathy—or even in money... The thought made her laugh again. She saw his look change slowly to perplexity. All his facial changes were slow, and she remembered, suddenly, how it had once diverted her to shift that lumbering scenery with a word. For the first time it struck her that she had been cruel. "There IS a question of help," she said in a softer key: "you can help me; but only by listening... I want to tell you something..."

Arment's resistance was not yielding. "Would it not be easier to—write?" he suggested.

She shook her head. "There is no time to write... and it won't take long." She raised her head and their eyes met. "My husband has left me," she said.

"Westall—?" he stammered, reddening again.

"Yes. This morning. Just as I left you. Because he was tired of me."

The words, uttered scarcely above a whisper, seemed to dilate to the limit of the room. Arment looked toward the door; then his embarrassed glance returned to Julia.

"I am very sorry," he said awkwardly.

"Thank you," she murmured.

"But I don't see—"

"No—but you will—in a moment. Won't you listen to me? Please!" Instinctively she had shifted her position putting herself between him and the door. "It happened this morning," she went on in short breathless phrases. "I never suspected anything—I thought we were—perfectly happy... Suddenly he told me he was tired of me... there is a girl he likes better... He has gone to her..." As she spoke, the lurking anguish rose upon her, possessing her once more to the exclusion of every other emotion. Her eyes ached, her throat swelled with it, and two painful tears burnt a way down her face.

Arment's constraint was increasing visibly. "This—this is very unfortunate," he began. "But I should say the law—"

"The law?" she echoed ironically. "When he asks for his freedom?"

"You are not obliged to give it."

"You were not obliged to give me mine—but you did."

He made a protesting gesture.

"You saw that the law couldn't help you—didn't you?" she went on. "That is what I see now. The law represents material rights—it can't go beyond. If we don't recognize an inner law... the obligation that love creates... being loved as well as loving... there is nothing to prevent our spreading ruin unhindered... is there?" She raised her head plaintively, with the look of a bewildered child. "That is what I see now... what I wanted to tell you. He leaves me because he's tired... but I was not tired; and I don't understand why he is. That's the dreadful part of it—the not understanding: I hadn't realized what it meant. But I've been thinking of it all day, and things have come back to me—things I hadn't noticed... when you and I..." She moved closer to him, and fixed her eyes on his with the gaze that tries to reach beyond words. "I see now that YOU didn't understand—did you?"

Their eyes met in a sudden shock of comprehension: a veil seemed to be lifted between them. Arment's lip trembled.

"No," he said, "I didn't understand."

She gave a little cry, almost of triumph. "I knew it! I knew it! You wondered—you tried to tell me—but no words came... You saw your life falling in ruins... the world slipping from you... and you couldn't speak or move!"

She sank down on the chair against which she had been leaning. "Now I know—now I know," she repeated.

"I am very sorry for you," she heard Arment stammer.

She looked up quickly. "That's not what I came for. I don't want you to be sorry. I came to ask you to forgive me... for not understanding that YOU didn't understand... That's all I wanted to say." She rose with a vague sense that the end had come, and put out a groping hand toward the door.

Arment stood motionless. She turned to him with a faint smile.

"You forgive me?"

"There is nothing to forgive—"

"Then will you shake hands for good-by?" She felt his hand in hers: it was nerveless, reluctant.

"Good-by," she repeated. "I understand now."

She opened the door and passed out into the hall. As she did so, Arment took an impulsive step forward; but just then the footman, who was evidently alive to his obligations, advanced from the background to let her out. She heard Arment fall back. The footman threw open the door, and she found herself outside in the darkness.

THE END OF THE RECKONING

VERSE

BOTTICELLI'S MADONNA IN THE LOUVRE.

WHAT strange presentiment, O Mother, lies
   On thy waste brow and sadly-folded lips,
   Forefeeling the Light's terrible eclipse
On Calvary, as if love made thee wise,
And thou couldst read in those dear infant eyes
   The sorrow that beneath their smiling sleeps,
   And guess what bitter tears a mother weeps
When the cross darkens her unclouded skies?

Sad Lady, if some mother, passing thee,
   Should feel a throb of thy foreboding pain,
   And think—"My child at home clings so to me,
With the same smile... and yet in vain, in vain,
Since even this Jesus died on Calvary"—
Say to her then: "He also rose again."

THE TOMB OF ILARIA GIUNIGI.

ILARIA, thou that wert so fair and dear
   That death would fain disown thee, grief made wise

With prophecy thy husband's widowed eyes
And bade him call the master's art to rear
Thy perfect image on the sculptured bier,
With dreaming lids, hands laid in peaceful guise
Beneath the breast that seems to fall and rise,
And lips that at love's call should answer, "Here!"

First-born of the Renascence, when thy soul
Cast the sweet robing of the flesh aside,
Into these lovelier marble limbs it stole,
Regenerate in art's sunrise clear and wide
As saints who, having kept faith's raiment whole,
Change it above for garments glorified.

THE SONNET.

PURE form, that like some chalice of old time
  Contain'st the liquid of the poet's thought
  Within thy curving hollow, gem-enwrought
  With interwoven traceries of rhyme,
While o'er thy brim the bubbling fancies climb,
  What thing am I, that undismayed have sought
  To pour my verse with trembling hand untaught
  Into a shape so small yet so sublime?

Because perfection haunts the hearts of men,
 Because thy sacred chalice gathered up
 The wine of Petrarch, Shakspere, Shelley—then
Receive these tears of failure as they drop
 (Sole vintage of my life), since I am fain
 To pour them in a consecrated cup.

TWO BACKGROUNDS.

I. LA VIERGE AU DONATEUR.
HERE by the ample river's argent sweep,
Bosomed in tilth and vintage to her walls,
A tower-crowned Cybele in armored sleep
The city lies, fat plenty in her halls,
With calm, parochial spires that hold in fee
The friendly gables clustered at their base,
And, equipoised o'er tower and market-place,
The Gothic minster's winged immensity;
And in that narrow burgh, with equal mood,
Two placid hearts, to all life's good resigned,
Might, from the altar to the lych-gate, find
Long years of peace and dreamless plenitude.
II. MONA LISA.
Yon strange blue city crowns a scarped steep

No mortal foot hath bloodlessly essayed;
Dreams and illusions beacon from its keep,
But at the gate an Angel bares his blade;
And tales are told of those who thought to gain
At dawn its ramparts; but when evening fell
Far off they saw each fading pinnacle
Lit with wild lightnings from the heaven of pain;
Yet there two souls, whom life's perversities
Had mocked with want in plenty, tears in mirth,
Might meet in dreams, ungarmented of earth,
And drain Joy's awful chalice to the lees.

EXPERIENCE.

I.

LIKE Crusoe with the bootless gold we stand
Upon the desert verge of death, and say:
"What shall avail the woes of yesterday
To buy to-morrow's wisdom, in the land
Whose currency is strange unto our hand?
In life's small market they have served to pay
Some late-found rapture, could we but delay
Till Time hath matched our means to our demand."

But otherwise Fate wills it, for, behold,
Our gathered strength of individual pain,
When Time's long alchemy hath made it gold,
Dies with us—hoarded all these years in vain,
Since those that might be heir to it the mould
Renew, and coin themselves new griefs again.

II.

O, Death, we come full-handed to thy gate,
Rich with strange burden of the mingled years,
Gains and renunciations, mirth and tears,
And love's oblivion, and remembering hate,
Nor know we what compulsion laid such freight
Upon our souls—and shall our hopes and fears
Buy nothing of thee, Death? Behold our wares,
And sell us the one joy for which we wait.
Had we lived longer, life had such for sale,
With the last coin of sorrow purchased cheap,
But now we stand before thy shadowy pale,
And all our longings lie within thy keep—
Death, can it be the years shall naught avail?

"Not so," Death answered, "they shall purchase sleep."

CHARTRES.

I.

IMMENSE, august, like some Titanic bloom,
  The mighty choir unfolds its lithic core,
Petalled with panes of azure, gules and or,
  Splendidly lambent in the Gothic gloom,
And stamened with keen flamelets that illume
  The pale high-altar. On the prayer-worn floor,
By surging worshippers thick-thronged of yore,
  A few brown crones, familiars of the tomb,
The stranded driftwood of Faith's ebbing sea—
  For these alone the finials fret the skies,
The topmost bosses shake their blossoms free,
  While from the triple portals, with grave eyes,
Tranquil, and fixed upon eternity,
  The cloud of witnesses still testifies.

II.

The crimson panes like blood-drops stigmatize
  The western floor. The aisles are mute and cold.
A rigid fetich in her robe of gold
  The Virgin of the Pillar, with blank eyes,
Enthroned beneath her votive canopies,
  Gathers a meagre remnant to her fold.
The rest is solitude; the church, grown old,
  Stands stark and gray beneath the burning skies.

Wellnigh again its mighty frame-work grows
   To be a part of nature's self, withdrawn
From hot humanity's impatient woes;
   The floor is ridged like some rude mountain lawn,
And in the east one giant window shows
   The roseate coldness of an Alp at dawn.

LIFE.

LIFE, like a marble block, is given to all,
A blank, inchoate mass of years and days,
Whence one with ardent chisel swift essays
Some shape of strength or symmetry to call;
One shatters it in bits to mend a wall;
One in a craftier hand the chisel lays,
And one, to wake the mirth in Lesbia's gaze,
Carves it apace in toys fantastical.

But least is he who, with enchanted eyes
Filled with high visions of fair shapes to be,
Muses which god he shall immortalize
In the proud Parian's perpetuity,
Till twilight warns him from the punctual skies
That the night cometh wherein none shall see.

AN AUTUMN SUNSET

I.

LEAGUERED in fire
The wild black promontories of the coast extend
Their savage silhouettes;
The sun in universal carnage sets,
And, halting higher,
The motionless storm-clouds mass their sullen threats,
Like an advancing mob in sword-points penned,
That, balked, yet stands at bay.
Mid-zenith hangs the fascinated day
In wind-lustrated hollows crystalline,
A wan valkyrie whose wide pinions shine
Across the ensanguined ruins of the fray,
And in her lifted hand swings high o'erhead,
Above the waste of war,
The silver torch-light of the evening star
Wherewith to search the faces of the dead.

II.

Lagooned in gold,
Seem not those jetty promontories rather
The outposts of some ancient land forlorn,
Uncomforted of morn,
Where old oblivions gather,

203

The melancholy, unconsoling fold
Of all things that go utterly to death
And mix no more, no more
With life's perpetually awakening breath?
Shall Time not ferry me to such a shore,
Over such sailless seas,
To walk with hope's slain importunities
In miserable marriage? Nay, shall not
All things be there forgot,
Save the sea's golden barrier and the black
Closecrouching promontories?
Dead to all shames, forgotten of all glories,
Shall I not wander there, a shadow's shade,
A spectre self-destroyed,
So purged of all remembrance and sucked back
Into the primal void,
That should we on that shore phantasmal meet
I should not know the coming of your feet?